David Newport

Pleasures of Home and Other Poems

David Newport

Pleasures of Home and Other Poems

ISBN/EAN: 9783744710381

Printed in Europe, USA, Canada, Australia, Japan

Cover: Foto ©Andreas Hilbeck / pixelio.de

More available books at **www.hansebooks.com**

THE

PLEASURES OF HOME

AND

OTHER POEMS.

BY

DAVID NEWPORT.

———

PHILADELPHIA:
J. B. LIPPINCOTT & CO.
1884.

PREFACE.

THE major part of these poems have been published heretofore ; they now constitute one volume.

Poetry is said to be a criticism of Life, and all true criticism means recompense or adjustment.

If any sentiment in this volume shall tend, in any mind, toward a recompense and right adjustment of life, the object of the author of this book will have been attained.

D. N.

ABINGTON, PENNSYLVANIA, 5th Mo. 1st, 1884.

CONTENTS.

TO AN AGNOSTIC FRIEND.

AND thou dost not know high heaven is good?
How strange! 'Tis my daily food.
How clear that human mind was made to know,
To know and feel the overflow
Of graciousness from Fountain source!
How wondrous strange, then, this divorce
Of consciousness from depth of feeling,
And Reason from Truth's high revealing!
As starlight from yon distant orb
Moves through ethereal realms superb,
So light supernal doth illuminate
The human mind and heart and permeate
Man's being. And thou dost not know
The Hand that doth thus graciously bestow
These marvels seen in sunlight and in star,
These harmonies which pulsate without a jar
Throughout the realms of thought divine?
Infinite and eternal, they doth incline
The list'ning ear and heark'ning sense
To highest, holiest eminence,—
To Mount of Vision, where transcendent shine
Those virtues which by tentative design
Transfigure garments white with light
And beauty. Oh, these should be thy heart's delight!
And thou dost not know and feel the eminence
Of Man? Thou hast no evidence
Of immortality?—of life beyond the grave?
And yet thou grantest that we have

In material things a Force and Power
Which binds with might and makes secure
All foundations,—that from tiniest stone
To distant star is o'erthrown
A law supremely grand and wise.
Secure thou stand'st here, and doth immortalize
Material things which transcend thy scope
Of mind.   Yes, thou say'st here, no hope
Has science e'er to scan the little or the great
By microscopic lens, or erst create
Vision telescopic which shall scan
The ultimate in particle from meanest thing to Man.
The ultimate is hid, thou sayest, in Nature's plan ;
Atomic force doth bind the warp and woof
Of Nature's frame, each particle aloof,
Distant, and separate, and yet are one
In unity, as scientists have clearly shown.
Each particle in itself a world of wonder,
Each atom revolving in its sphere, and under
All a power and marvel that doth bespeak
A plan.   No pause, no failure, not a break.
In all the marvellous, wondrous chain that bind
In bonds eternal the great or little not an end
Is seen.   In microscopic objects sphere fits to sphere,
Atom to atom, in liquids, solids, or in atmosphere.
As in the little, so the great, in smallest speck or Pleaid
        grand,
All things bespeak the Infinite: the mind of man, a grain of
        sand !
In Nature's crucible divinest alchemy is known ;
Her book of many pages has an Index one.
All is infinite, and hath proceeded from and doth revolve
Around the Infinite again, unfold, disclose, evolve
Again, in endless circuit, 'round the central sphere,
Transforming and transcending, thus all things cohere.
Units of sodium in that distant sphere

Rhythm keep and concert with their kindred units
    here,
And brightest hue of sunset thus appear :
'Tis caused by kindred drops thus mingling into one.
Thus space is spanned by yonder distant sun,
And so elastic the ethereal wave
That binds all space that it seems to have
A solid base, wherein intelligence doth tread
The labyrinth's maze, and weave the hidden thread
Of spiritual beauty, high Heaven's appeal.
But " thou canst not speak of that thou dost not feel."
Be silent then ; love Solitude, and court
The Muse. Let lucid calm be thy resort
From crudeness, and from skeptic's doubt
Within thy soul, within thy heart, and not without !
E'en thou canst read the Book of Life aright
E'en thou canst trace the lines of living light
In Truth's gospel. Glad tidings these indeed
To many a mind enfranchised, whom she has freed.
And origin of man thou wouldst solve ?
And yet so ignorant that thou canst not evolve
A sense, or disconnect from common weal
The good of all ! Herein doth Heaven high reveal,
Make known to Man, concensus clear,
Her voice to all : 'tis ever near.
Yes, here again is unity disclosed,—
A law of sympathy and love which flows
As river of our peace. Graciousness to man
Is Heaven's high law. With this he can span
The arch which binds the universe,
Traverse all space, and in his heart rehearse
A song of sweetness and a hymn of praise.
Thus he can raise in scale of being, all his ways
Attuned to Nature's law, he pleased with her and she
    with him.
O thou of little faith, thus thou shalt climb

The sacred stairway,—not as they at Vatican,
With mind benumbed by superstitious bane ;
But, as Luther, thou shalt lean upon the staff of Faith,
And with fidelity and trust in Her.   The zenith
Of thy life and power shall consecrated be
To elevate the truth and make men free.
Unless the Human seeks thus his degree
" He withers at the heart, and looks as wan
As the pale spectre of a murdered man."
And what is Truth ?   Dost thou aspire
By sight and sense ?   Dost thou inquire
By sensuous cetera the truth, the life, the way ?
And thou art learned, and knowest the essay
Of science,—how she chasm deep hath found,
How her ripest and her wisest seers expound
The truth.   They have no thought, no dream, no hope
To bridge the gulf.   'Tis utterly beyond the scope
Of Man to tell how life and thought doth animate
The world.   Too high, too deep, too broad, too great
The mystery of life, of thought, of mind, to solve,—
Too great for man to tell.   It doth involve
All motion.   How the senseless brain, dull and inanimate,
Is lit with high intelligence, surpassing great !
Themes transcendent high doth show an outer
And an inner world.   High Heaven—can we doubt her ?—
Hath a realm of feeling wherein we know,
Because we feel, her bounteous overflow.
That feeds and satisfies the inward sense
With clearest, purest evidence !
Sum up the love all human hearts have ever known,
Count all, in every land, 'neath every zone,—
'Tis but the love of Heaven for her own !
Thus Love was born,—and Love can never die,—
Celestial origin divine, Humanity doth testify.
And as is mother's love for dearest son,
So Heavenly Love doth look upon

Her offspring. From womb of Love, Perseus, thou hast
    sprung.
A Heavenly Love that's careless of its young?
Oh, thou agnostic disputant, who doth grant
Eternity to matter, how extravagant, how ignorant
Thou art thus in thy philosophy to give
Eternity to senseless things, and love and mind as fugitive!
Thou sayest it matters not; thou shalt survive and live.
Proceeding from the Eternal font sublime,
Thou shalt survive thy foolish crime
Of doubt and disbelief. Thou yet shall see
The Truth, her beauty; she will make thee free.
Thou yet shall see in clearest light
E'en here below. Renew'd shall be thy sight;
Thy heart shall live by that thy lips disown;
Thy trust shall be in Wisdom's ways alone.
Ne'er shalt thou speak of Her as the unknown;
For now, and here, our eyes doth see
Those portals which reveal Eternity.

THE PLEASURES OF HOME.

I.

PROFOUNDEST feeling that o'erflows the heart,
Immortalized by song and crowned by art!
To thee the minstrel full oft his harp will tune,
For in thy paths are flowers of fancy strewn.
A Burns has wandered in those paths along
With heart inspired, attuned to glowing song,
For Scotia's homes, the dearest and the best,
In vales sequestered, on the mountain's crest.
Or where, O poet-peasant, thou hast discoursed beside,
Or watched with kindling glance, the Yarrow's silver tide;
Or where thy "Mary in heaven" whispered to the soul
Of melody, as gentle Ayr without control;
Or 'neath the shades that deck thy banks, O bonnie Doon.
Such scenes, they are embalmed in Scottish hearts as flowers
        of June;
And while gliding o'er the wild Atlantic's wave,
Or where Pacific's surges peaceful lave,
Tho' o'er wooded heights, o'er vast prairies roam,
Still by Scotland's sons are treasured thoughts of home.

And tho' from native land by rugged shores exiled,
Thy songs, O Burns, have oft the exile's heart beguiled:
They thrill the soul and spring spontaneous from the tongue.
Yes, all o'er the world thy glowing songs are sung;
And none, tho' wreathed in chaplets set in glory,
Or chanting forth of much-loved Highland story,

Tho' chiming sweet in matchless tome,
None touch the heart like songs of home.
The wanderer sings of Auld Lang Syne
O'er roaring seas, 'neath clustering vine ;
Where'er he wanders, where'er he be,
His frequent thoughts they turn to thee.
For as magnet points to polar star,
So love doth wander oft afar
To earliest scenes on native soil ;
'Round these Affection's tendrils coil.

Can these emotions e'er transported be,
As from native land the cultured tree?
No ; not without a wrench of roots below.
The tree may wither, or, perchance, may grow,
May flourish, if beneath a genial clime,
May grow and blossom in some fruitful time ;
But ne'er can time or clime efface
Or change the nature or the race.
The tree will e'er its foreign growth attest,
So Man can ne'er his earliest thoughts repress.
Another generation must adorn the stage,
The current alter and mind engage.

II.

Ask of the patriot from dear France an exile,
Tho' the orange may blossom and the seasons may smile ;
Tho' spices and balm on the wings of the gale ;
Tho' the flowers of the tropics their fragrance exhale ;
Tho' clouds fringed with gold thus drape the sky ;
Tho' the breath of the zephyr be soft as a sigh ;
Tho' sweet-ladened odors and grateful perfume ;.
Tho' the summer in beauty, in glory may bloom ;
Yet that land to the exile is naught but a tomb.

He dreams of dear France, his loved native shore.
On Memory's swift wing Imagination doth soar,
And mirrors the treasures which are stored in the mind,
Speaking of kindred, which to native strand bind,
The home of his fathers, his childhood's dear home.
'Midst the scenes of the past sweet Fancy doth roam,—
The bower in the garden 'neath the clambering vine,
On the banks of the Seine, or the slopes of the Rhine.
He thinks of sweet Home, where in boyhood he played
In the old orchard, 'neath the apple-tree shade ;
Of the wine-press which, at each wrench of the lever,
Gave forth in red streams to the iron-bound receiver
The streams of that nectar, which oft he had quaff'd,
As pure as the love in his bosom engraft,—
The love of his youth, that bright radiant star,
Which shone o'er his life and beamed from afar.
He thought of the minstrel and the oft merry dance,
Of the note of the lute, 'neath the olive of France.
He thought of the vineyard, where oft he had trod ;
Of the cross at the altar, dedicated to God ;
Of the shrine of the Virgin, where his fathers oft knelt,
And as balm to the soul her sweet presence felt.
'Twas there he plighted his faith, the love of his youth,
His heart and his hand,—the seal of his truth.

For dear France he sighs on Cayenne's dread shore,
And curses the tyrant who from native land tore.*
His vow he renews to loved liberty plighted,
The despot disowned, and fair Freedom righted.
Such prayers as these are on western winds borne
From the heart of the exile, drear and forlorn.
They speed o'er the ocean, are heard in the gales
That waft o'er the deep and fill the white sails.

---

* In treachery and cruelty, Louis Napoleon was a fitting successor to his great uncle.

What was the crime that from native land banished?
Why were these patriots of loved liberty ravished?
This the crime they committed, for this warr'd in their might:
The usurper they hated, and struck for the right,
For home and the fireside, that sacred domain;
These, man's dearest rights, they strove to maintain;
Their country they loved, and vowed to defend her.
For this their heart's tendrils were thus torn asunder.

Just Heaven! how long is the despot to reign?
How long from just vengeance will thy legions refrain?
How long will Truth's martyrs in dungeons be cast?
Are such scenes forever, forever to last?
Must Freedom lurk in the mountain and hide in the cave?
Never gird on her armor the tyrant to brave?
Shall her cause never conquer, ne'er her banner unfurl?
And the despot, exulting, reign over the world?
All over but 'neath fair Columbia's sky,
Her arms only open for the patriot to fly;
Only her forest a refuge, her wild plains a home,
Where the wild locust blossoms and the prairie-rose bloom.

Must Liberty perish, by brute force overcome,
And behind the horizon set forever her sun?
Not forever, tho' it may seem long delayed,
That time for which oft the patriot has prayed.
Her march to her empire to us may seem slow,
That her rills gather slowly, that her torrents ne'er flow;
But a year unto her, 'tis but as a day,—
Time she measureth not as it floweth away.
She knows that her kingdom at last it will come
To gladden the heart, to gladden the Home!

III.

O Home, much-loved Home, the heart's dearest treasure,
Of affection and kindred the sacred enclosure,

Universal thy pleasures, in every clime known,
The same o'er the wide world, in every zone!
The savage he loves thee, on bear-skin reclining;
The slave as he toils is for native land pining;
The soldier in battle, his last thought is of thee,
And he battles the braver if his home 'tis to free.
The merchant gains gold and vends in the mart,
The future he hopes for 'tis Home's magic art;
The sailor as he peers o'er the boundless horizon,
The lark as she sings from the meadow arising;
Toward home on high crag the eagle is soaring,
Tho' the lightning is near and the torrent is pouring,
Yet, poised on his wing, he wends on his way,
With the salmon he wrenched from the fish-hawk away.
This he bears in his talons to the mountain's high crest,
There by beak of his eaglets with affection caressed.
The whelp of the lion, their fierce sire purring round,
He fondles them gently as he reclines on the ground.
Thus 'tis not only to Man is Home a sweet rest,
But the fox has his hole, the wild bird a nest.

Ofttimes has Ambition relinquished the prize,
The goal which she saw in the prospect arise,
And strove to embrace as Hope's fond fruition.
But, disenchanted by nearness, lo! the transition
When pursuit is abandoned, when sated by honor,
When glory ne'er dazzles, when wearied by splendor,
The king has descended, disrobed and dethroned!
The warrior and statesman have glory disowned,
And sought those endearments in affection's rich mine,
Those pleasures and treasures which e'er radiant shine,
Which throw over life's shadows a rich mellow ray,
Illuming our pilgrimage and cheering the way.
Yes, first at the cradle the infant to greet,
Then a mother watches o'er us and lulls to slumbers sweet.

Every smile 'tis noted, 'tis treasured in the heart,
And every grief 'tis vanquished by a mother's magic art.
Thus lovelight on earth and lovelight from heaven
Are freely bestowed and generously given.
From Orion'and Pleiad they flow bright and free,
As an earnest, O Man, is homelight to thee.
Then banish the shadows which over thee roll,
With light in the stars and with trust in thy soul !

IV.

Hail ! heavenly beacon.   Since darkness erst fled
Wast ever on Man greater happiness shed ?
Wast ever since Creation's anthem first was sung,
Since o'er shapeless void our earth was swung,
Since solar ray first dazzling glowed
And banished darkness on its road
Through space, since chaos burst into birth
Wast ever known on God's green earth—
Wast ever known 'neath Heaven's high dome—
Joys greater than the joys of Home ?
Banished be every bliss in human heart,
But, oh ! let not the rays of Home depart !
Let these but linger and console the mind,
Some solace still the heart can find.
Let, O let Affection's fingers touch the trembling strings,
The cords which bind the soul to earthly things !
Let Love's sweet solace but attune the lyre,
Life's ills are soothed, fulfilled each fond desire.
This, only this can constant bliss supply ;
This, only this can shine beatific in Life's sky .
Then glow, ye orbs ! shed, shed your rays.
Ye heavenly lamps, that lustrous blaze
O'erhead, light, light us on our way !
And tell, O tell, doth in Heaven's eternal day,

Do these affections which inspire the heart below,
Which deepen like the streamlets as they flow,
Oh, in that bright world, that circling seat of bliss,
Lives human love? glows earthly happiness?
Do those twining plants that cling so closely here,
Do they exist in Heaven's immortal sphere?

I singled out a star that twinkled in the sky,
And, enraptured, gazed till methought I had reply,—
Love, 'tis of God: it can never, never die!

Pleased with the thought, the inspiring thought,
That to my heart such welcome brought,—
Yes, it nerved my soul, my wish to share
Those heavenly joys that bloom immortal there.

And that thrilling word, from twinkling star above,
Dost not accord with what we know of love,
Of friendship, and those soothing social ties
Which beam at Home with lustrous eyes?

Yes, when Love from heaven to earth descended,
'Twas by angelic hosts attended.
They breathed in Man celestial fire,
Attuned the harp and strung the lyre.
In chorus to the heavenly choir,
In anthems blending with the notes,
In concert with the air that floats,
That radiant glows with halo bright,
Fills heavenly halls with amber light,—
Those halls of bliss in spheres above,—
Resplendent beam with angel's love!
'Tis love emblazons 'round the Throne,
Encircling o'er though space 'tis thrown;
Attracting souls and knitting hearts,
Its magic ray to mind imparts!

'Twill circle thus in endless years,
'Twill gleam amidst revolving spheres ;
'Twill elevate from earthly dross,
'Twill throw its radiant light across
Unnumbered worlds! 'Twill Man inspire
With thoughts beyond all low desire,
'Twill glow till Love majestic reigns,
'Twill bind with amaranthine chains !
'Twill blend its grace in every face,
'Twill change and beautify the race,
'Twill circuit till God's worlds become
Emblazoned in the rays of Home !

V.

Columbia's *pater patriæ*, oft tired of war and state parade,
Longed, loved Vernon, for thy umbrageous shade ;
And tho' Freedom's clarion notes oft urged to deadly war,
The beacon-light of Home, that was the cherished star.
And when liberty 'twas won, when the hero's strife was o'er,
How wishfully he looked to thee, Potomac's pebbled shore !
How anxiously expectant when he led his legions on !
Oh, who was like to thee, Columbia's Washington ?
Who, when the victory won, when Freedom's rights restored,
Willingly—nay, ardently—preferred the ploughshare to the
 sword.
Had an empire's crown been offered, he would the bribe
 have spurned,
And the more lovingly toward sweet Home have turned.
Oh, much to thee, fair Freedom, didst this glowing love impart ;
Much mayst thou thank, O Liberty, it filled thy hero's heart,—
That in that patriot's pulses the love of country throbbed,
That Home encircled round him, that Virtue sat enrobed.

VI.

Aristæus, son of Apollo, with sweets thou didst flavor
The fruits, and taught unto Man their delicate savor ;

But ere he tasted of them he'd felt the sweet joys of Home.
Adam's heart knew these when o'er the garden he'd roam,—
Not perfected, indeed, until Eve he was given:
'Twas then Eden blossomed with joys as of heaven.
Oh, what is the bliss, and where are the flowers
That compare with sweet Home 'neath her eglantine bowers?
Dost say that Hope, fair enchantress, more joy e'er combine,
More of beauty and grace in her hawthorn entwine?

O goddess propitious! there's a snare in thy art;
Deferred thy felicity, thou sickeneth the heart.
Thou art as Apollo at Delphi's shrines:
At times thou honoreth, but oft hope repines.
The wayworn pilgrim, as he surmounts thy high towers,
Will expectant remain in thy turrets many, many drear hours.

O beautiful illusion, that glimmereth anon,
Thy ray 'tis but fancied; when grasped for, 'tis gone!
Thou promiseth Youth a glorious career.
He looketh to thee; he sees naught to fear.
Ambition and Genius, they go hand in hand;
Hope glitters before them with her magical wand.
She leadeth the way; she beckoneth on.
Youth follows rejoicing, with music and song;
But the laurel he sees, to encircle his brow.
With his foot in the furrow, his hand on the plough,
He glanceth not back: he believeth in thee.
At thy shrine he worshippeth; there bendeth the knee.
Thy form 'tis refulgent, adorned with beauty and grace;
It encircles thy brow and beams in thy face.

But is not thy face deceitful and siren thy tongue?
Hast thou not misled with the song thou hast sung?
From home and the fireside, happy and bright,
Hast thou not allured with thy Will-o'-wisp light?

And Youth oft hast promised, with thy smile so enticing ?
Seducing his heart, with thy gentle surmising,
From the home of his childhood, the home of his youth.
Thou hast oft decoyed him from honor and truth,
Attracting and luring from Contentment's sweet vales,
To launch on Life's ocean and spread all his sails.

Take from Hope the pleasures of Home,
Of country and kindred, how altered her tome !
How tamed is her soaring, how joyless her aim !
Tell me not of ambition, the glories of fame ;
Tell me not of Johnson, of Goldsmith, or Gray,
Of Chatham, Burke, Sheridan, Webster, or Clay ;
Refer me not to Homer, Petrarch, Shakespeare, or Milton,
To Bacon, Copernicus, Galileo, Harvey, or Newton ;
Quote not to me of e'en great or illustrious man,
I tell you that life is at best but a span ;
That fame's an illusion, a bauble, a cheat ;
That ambition and glory both at the grave meet.
Oh, thousands on thousands have knelt at their shrine.
Youth ! hast thou imagined greatness was thine ?
Where now are the laurels thou thoughtst to twine,
To twine 'round thy brow, o'er the ages to shine ?
Are they not trampled to earth, and forgotten long since ?
Thy name and thy lineage gone, O whence ?
And silence repeated and slow echoed back.
No trace can I find, no time-honored track,—
The grave and its shadows have closed over thy dust ;
The name thou so vauntest, 'tis covered with rust.

Inquirest thou, then, is there no happiness here ?
Is life, then, so dreary, so o'erburdened with care ?
Is hope an illusion, imagination a dream ?
Is the sun of youth's longing never, never to beam ?
Is earth but a vast grave, drear and forlorn ?
Was Man made and created only to mourn ?

Not so! Look thou at the first flush of morn ;
See the beauties of earth that thy pathway adorn ;
Watch the mist on the river, slow lifting its curtain.
Repine not in thy heart, there are joys which are certain.
Walk forth in the fields ; hear the music around thee,—
The sweet warbling of birds, the hum of the bee.
O'erhead view the canopy that circles thee 'round ;
Listen to Nature, hear the melodious sound.
Watch thy heart-beatings, thy soul-promptings within,
Thou wilt see that thy soul was ne'er fashioned for sin.

VII.

Oh, come with me, friend, in the sweet vales of life,
Away from ambition, fame, glory, and strife ;
Come wander with me 'neath Heaven's high dome.
I'll sing of Contentment, the joys of sweet Home,
Of Peace, Virtue, and Sweetness,—those twin sisters three,—
Of Culture combined with true Liberty.
I'll lead you not to the city, tho' perchance there 'tis found,
But its conventionalisms fetter and bind the mind 'round
Too much to exhibit the pure pleasures of Home ;
So to Pennsylvania's loved manors, O thitherward come.
Come, come with me, friend, the theme it impels,
And Phœbus, she'd wander 'neath life's flow'ry dells ;
Pomona woos to orchards, to gardens, to a far-distant vale,
Where woodlands rich, where glist'ning dews prevail.
In grotto fair we'll seek some favors of those sisters nine,—
Mayhap a tranquil grace around our Muse they'll twine.
Some flow'ret sweet they'll give, perchance, that blossoms
     unseen,—
Some violet fair that hides, with artless, modest mien,
In forest dense or meadows green.
Such flowers there grow ; they scent the gale,
They bloom, they die, their fragrance they exhale !
Fair Thalia, such scenes I know thou too admires ;
For 'tis in the noiseless vales of life the Muse retires.

From bustle, glare, and fashion she withdraws;
O'ercome with noise, she sinks 'neath loud applause.

Drive the steed gently, now; let him rest there,
While we drink a pure draught and inhale the sweet air.
Look thou around thee, survey the rich scene!
See the dark, waving corn, the meadows so green.
Cast thy eye o'er the waters, o'er gentle Schuylkill:
Seest thou the smoke yonder, the smoke of the kiln,
Slow curling its columns beyond the reach of the eye?
Watch its dusky, vapory wreathings till lost in the sky.
Hear the splash of the water, the clang of the mill;
See the spire in the distance on the brow of the hill.
Was ever landscape more fair, more beauty conveyed?
Know'st thou prospect more rich?   Has eye ever surveyed?

There, just to the right of those tall poplar-trees,
That sway to and fro in the soft summer breeze,—
There, just over that bridge that circles so lightly,
There, there is a home where friendship beams brightly.
'Tis there, in that nook, lives my much-honored friend:
Thitherward (in thought), good steed, we will wend.
Thou smilest, friend, thou hollow-cheeked man,
And enviest that reaper, with his face bronzed with tan.
Well mayst thou envy him: there's content in his heart,
Whilst thy brain is busied with bonds in the mart.
See his broad swath through the trembling grain!
There's grace in his action and power in his aim;
There's health on his cheek, in his arm there is wealth,—
They are treasures far greater, friend, than thy golden pelf.
For such as he are at once our glory and pride,
And ne'er to Columbia can their place be supplied.
And woe to thee, Liberty, to the spoiler a prey!
Beware, O Columbia! beware of that day
When luxury and wealth shall o'er the land ride,
Engulfing our landmarks with their o'erflowing tide!

When corruption and falsehood shall rule o'er the land,
Shall marshal their forces and muster their band,
Seize the strongholds of state, and interpret the law,
Explaining freedom away by some legal flaw ;
When the Law, thus corrupted, be with *Faction* allied,
And the foul hand of Party the ship of state guide.
Cherish, then, O my country, men fresh from the field,—
Much less likely are they to corruption to yield.

That tan-embrowned man was a school-chum of mine.
We've trapped, fished, and hunted in youth's golden prime ;
Together we've wandered o'er these steep hills,
Caught the white-tailed rabbit, trolled for trout in the rills.
On the crest of that rock we oft used to climb,
Richly paid for our toil by the prospect sublime.
Oft we've traversed those woods and tracked the raccoon,
Went giging for pike with the mimic harpoon ;   ·
And with Rollo the faithful close in our rear,
Together we've chatted of panther and deer,
Giving wing to sweet Fancy, and imagined again
That the wild warrior roamed over mountain and plain.
We've heard the loud war-whoop, which the hills echoed back,
And saw the red man descend with death in his track.
We've fancied this, too, not without some plausible ground ;
For arrow-heads by the score in the valley we've found.
Those memorials of battle on the ground there were strewn,
And oft here and there we've found the axe of stone hewn.

Oh, dear is that river where in boyhood I've bathed !
Yes, oft in thy waters, O Schuylkill, I've laved ;
And oft with patience, too, along thy shore
The dipsy, net, and rod I've bore ;
And have list, enraptured, to the boatman's horn,
As o'er thy silvery waves the glad music was borne.
And this scraggy beech bears marks which endears,
For the name of the maiden with mine there appears.

She and I have went nutting ere the sun showed his face.
Ah, may those joyous days time never, never efface!
For oft fond memory revisits boyhood's loved scene,—
The forest, the river, the meadow so green.
Each nook in those rocks I knew them full well.
There an old hermit dwelt whom our fortunes would tell,—
Not as gypsy or crone, by e'en mystical plan ;
In the eye he would gaze and the countenance scan.
I've stood by his cave, chained with wondering ear ;
Have gazed in his face, with the oft trickling tear,
As he unburdened his sorrow, his trouble, his care.
On the banks of this river we were seated,—just there.
On the banks of sweet Schuylkill, on a moss-covered seat,
The reason he told why he sought that retreat,
Why from society thus secluded he lived in a cave,
Why banished from Home, 'neath Nature's architrave.
His heart's affections I knew were tender and true,
That his mind bespoke one,—a love of virtue.

With attention I listened. The old soldier began ;
He unfolded his life ; thus the theme ran :
" I was born," said he, " o'er the ocean, on the banks of the
        Tweed.
Ah ! when I think of my youth, it makes my heart bleed.
My father was a patriot on Scotia's dear shore.
Oh, oft in my mind the old home I explore,—
Tho' fourscore and six winters have made tresses gray,
Yet the stone from the well rolls quickly away,—
The cot on the banks of the swift-flowing Tweed,
The elm-tree before it on the closely-cropt mead.
Ah, now, with memory's aid, methinks I sit and see
My mother, as with her children she sat 'neath that glorious
        old tree.
'Twas oft she gathered us on the sweet Sabbath eve,
And read of the Christ, the counsel He gave ;

How He loved little children, and broke of the bread ;
How He gathered the multitude, the multitude fed.
My mother ! methinks I hear thy accents mild,
Methinks thou smil'st on thy child !
Alas ! 'tis but a shadow that my vision surveys,
'Tis but an illusion that fond memory portrays.
·Yet I love thus to linger o'er that much-cherished scene,
And as the grave yawns before me thus oft I dream.
When young," said the old man, "I was adventurous and
    wild.
Tho' my home was attractive, and a sweet sister smiled ;
Tho' a brother loving,—beloved,—gallant, and brave,
Yet this ne'er my longings restrained, ne'er from sad fortune
    could save ;
For I wished dearly to roam on the ocean of life,—
I loved scenes of excitement, ambition, and strife.
My father, therefore, gave me a portion ; I bade mother fare-
    well,
Clasped brother and sister.   Yes, I remember full well
The emotion within me on leaving dear native land.
But I sailed o'er the ocean for Columbia's famed strand.

Not long was I here ere War's clarion sounded,
That music I loved much.   Oh, how my heart bounded
When I heard the invader had crossed the deep sea
To 'slave the land that I lived in, to subdue liberty !
For I loved freedom at home, 'neath Scotia's bright sun ;
Had read of great Bruce, how country 'twas won;
Had heard of those times, how Wallace had toiled,
How England was vanquished and Edward was foiled ;
How our bonneted chieftains, with broadsword and spear,
Rushed to the battle with no thought of fear.
My father, he too was a warrior, and oft has he told
Of a grandsire of his, free, fearless, and bold.
Ne'er Scotland had chieftain more trusty or tried ;
For country he lived and for country he died.

Thus heroic blood within me pulsed through my youthful
    veins,
And I vow'd, as that patriot sire before me, to resist the
    . tyrant's chains,
And joined the patriot army where great Washington led.
Ah, my lad, how we suffered! how those patriots bled!
What a sweet prize is liberty! how much it has cost!
What treasure was lavished! oh, the lives that were lost!
Their sufferings, their trials never half has been told,—
What it cost your fathers loved freedom to mould.
My son, cherish that legacy, and to your children bequeath,
For 'tis our honor and glory, 'tis the old soldier's wreath;
'Tis yours and your children's, to guard it with care,
The heritage we've left you, rich, precious, and rare.

"Oh Thou!" said the old man, with his eyes raised to heaven,
"Guard, guard this loved land! Let thy blessing be given!
Guard Thou fair Freedom! for that was the prize.
To her the altar, to her the sacrifice!"
The old hero paused, with agitation overcome,
And recurred for a moment to his far-distant home.
I looked on his emotion as the weakness of age;
But I knew not what throbbed in the heart of the sage.
He soon mastered the feeling, and his narrative pursued
With mind much more calmed, with emotion subdued.
" I joined the patriots," said he, " and at Lexington fought,
In Canada with Arnold,—we there prodigies wrought,—
Was a dragoon of Lee's at famous Stillwater,—
A glorious day that for Freedom, though grievous the slaugh-
    ter.
My old commander, Arnold, there raged as one crazed.
Oh, much might his name be now honored and praised,
Might be valued by country, by kindred and kind,
And his fame with the cypress and myrtle be twin'd,
Had the dread Reaper garnered him on that bloody field!
But Fate urged him on, and dire Treason sealed.

A Washington generously trusted.   How was he repaid ?
Columbia was bartered and Freedom betrayed !
That man I loved much, tho' his faults I well knew,—
That his passions were strong, that his virtues were few.
Yet I ne'er shall forget on Quebec's high crest,
When the steel pressed my bosom with bayonet-thrust,
When the enemy were round me, my back to a wall,
Thus battling alone he rushed at my call.
Scattered quick were the foemen ; the confusion was dire ;
Blood-stained his sabre, his eye flashed with fire !
He was glorious in battle, then generous his heart.
'Twas gold and ambition, their terrible art,
'Twas hope disappointed, a mind naturally vain,
Splendor and show, a weak heart and brain,—
This led him a captive, this made him a slave,
Bowed his high name and dishonored his grave."

VIII.

" On Brandywine's disastrous field there I bore a part,
And witnessed on that dreadful field War's cruel, cruel art.
With my legion, too, at Germantown
I urged my steed, with broadsword drawn.
'Twas on the eve of that day, ere the moon filled her horn,
As, weary of contest, tired, sick, and forlorn,
As I paced with worn steed on the banks of this stream,
And watched with fond glance the moon's gentle beam,
A footfall I heard.   Nearer it came.
I urged my steed faster o'er the rough-beaten lane,
And struggled to reach the foot of the hill.
To hide in the alder that bordered the rill.
In my saddle I turned, saw my endeavor was vain ;
For my horse was hard travelled, sore-footed, and lame.
So broadsword I unsheathed, as thundering they came,
One after the other, the tallest before.
Like a torrent he rushed, as red-handed war.

The blood stirred within me, thro' my veins danced;
I thought not of fatigue as on he advanced.
But my steed moving wearily, I quickly turned round,
And horse and the rider they rolled on the ground.

" His companion rode up, his steed at full trot;
We rapidly charged, each exchanging a shot.
My horse fell beneath me, my combatant's the same.
Ah, had I but asked that opponent his name!
The moon was hid 'neath a cloud; not a word had been
        spoken
As broadsword crossed broadsword,—that the dire token,—
Blade upon blade, cross-cut and pass,
And blood, warm blood, soon trickled on the green growing
        grass.
Clang after clang broke the stillness of night,
Steel crossed steel, reflected the moon's silver light.
I tried all the sleights of my art known but to one,·
And he methought far away 'neath Scotia's fair sun.
Answered were all—cut for cut, thrust for thrust.
At last, oh! at last he—he—bit the dust!''

The old man again paused, and on his time-furrowed cheek
The tears coursed their way as he endeavored to speak;
For his emotions were stirred to the depths of his soul,
And some time elapsed ere his heart could control.
At last, with faltering utterance, he said,—
" There prostrate he lay, there prostrate he bled!
' Friend,' queried the dying man,—'twas the first word he had
        spoken,—
' Where learned you your art?' said he, in accent quite
        broken.
Like lightning it flashed; I rushed to his side:
' O Robert, my brother, stay! Stay, O life's tide!
Accursed, oh! accursed be that fatal blow
That laid thee, my darling, my loved one, so low!'

Thus frantic I acted, thus frantic I spoke.
His head backward fell: his heart too was broke.
The recognition 'twas mutual, as ray follows ray,
As light gushes forth from the great font of day.
From my canteen I gave him, drop by drop, the cool water;
I prayed him to speak, but not a word did he utter.
His temples I chafed as he lay in death's trance;
Once he opened his eyes,—oh, the love in that glance!
'Twas pity and tenderness that beamed in his eye.
In my arms, on my bosom, he breathed his last sigh,
Just here where we siti   I wept o'er his remains,
And earnestly wished death would release my heart-pains.
Oh, the agony, the heart-crushing agony I felt,
As by the side of my brother, my dead brother, I knelt!
A comrade extended his sympathy and aid:
We buried him just there with the mattock and spade.
By that juniper there he fell, there lies his dust;
His spirit is in Heaven, thus humbly I trust.
My son," said the old man, " promise me this—
'Tis all that I ask—'tis nothing amiss:
In that day which is coming,—to me 'twill be soon,—
By the side of my brother, let that be my tomb.
There, 'neath the shade of that sycamore-tree,
Promise, my son, there my sepulchre shall be."

I promised the old man, and homeward I went.
My heart was much touched, by sympathy rent.
On the morrow, toward the hermit's cave I again turned
       my face.
Alas! there he lay in Death's cold embrace.
Fond neighbors gathered, and 'neath the wide-spreading tree
There his body we laid—his spirit was free.

IX.

But here are we, near my friend's farm.
Faster, faster, good steed, and save us from harm;

For the thunder is rolling, a storm distant looms.
This, friend, is one of Pennsylvania's fair homes.
In his house we'll find a welcome hospitable,
Cheer and comfort for self, for our steeds a good stable.
Trees, you perceive, they are planted with taste ;
In orchard and lawn with art they are placed.
And his fields, you observe, with great care are tilled,
For his mind 'tis artistic, in husbandry skilled.
Their appearance (says he) 'tis the garnisher of thought,
And the uses are graces, tho' rough hands have wrought.
Thus utility and beauty should e'er be combined,—
The ivy and oak,—as in the well ordered min l.
Oft he points to the heavens, to the beauties of Nature,—
How the landscape 'tis furnished with eye-pleasing verdure ;
That all objects evolving some beauty disclose ;
That the briery stem is the stem of the rose.
Thus knowledge objective to Man is conveyed
In the wisdom and beauty in Nature displayed.
And subjective knowledge, as the essence of thought,
In the mind of the seer is welded and wrought ;
And twain become one in the travail of birth,
As heaven is brought from the skies to our earth.
Good friend, good steed, this lane we will enter
In fancy,—'twas all that I promised, the Muse should be mentor
That she's coy and uncertain I need not rehearse,
Oft confounding the poet and confounding his verse.
And so oft quacks have woo'd her, 'tis almost a crime
To jingle in verse or to reason in rhyme.
Let the critic, then, guard with his terrible skill,
For his trade, as the doctor's, 'tis to cure or to kill.
This gate we will ope,—'tis the home of my friend,—
With no fear in the mind 'twill his privacy offend.
Look around and observe the neatness and order,
The trees in the lane that range on the border.
Look o'er the fence : the sod, how nicely prepared ;
The clover and timothy evenly mixed in the sward.

See the kine in the meadow, in the stream to their knees,
There chewing their cud and enjoying the breeze.
In contemplation they seem lost while preparing their store,
The ambrosial delicious which they contentedly pour
Into the pail of the maiden,—that nectarous draught,
That golden luxury which fair hands have wrought.

The corn 'tis just tassel'd, just showing the ear;
The crop has been nurtured and cultured with care.
Its future 'tis now left to good fences and heaven,
That the showers of July may be plenteously given.
For mowing times over, the tall timothy gathered,
The wheat 'tis all stacked, and the gleanings are garnered,
And the farmers all ready and anxious for showers
To revive the parched plants and nourish the flowers,
Noting each change, each rumbling of thunder,
Querying of neighbor, Will it rain, I much wonder?
O Rain! thou art a commodity sadly abused;
And as for predicting thy vapors, 'tis confusion confused.
In foul weather thou rain'st without the least trouble;
But when raining's ne'er the fashion, the thunders may rumble,
The lightnings may flash, but ne'er a drop doth appear.
Thou art sadly abused, 'specially in the spring of the year;
But in the heat of July thou rejoiceth the farmers,
Thou gladdens their hearts, put'th corn in their garners.

The farmers are now engaged in that rich mine of gold,
The barnyard manure, with its treasures untold.
This they're hauling and spreading, for the wheat crop pre-
       paring,
And no expense, toil, or trouble they're sparing.
The glebe is broke twice and tilled with great care
Ere, O generous Mother, generative and fair,
Erst the seed is committed to thy bounteous breast,
Fondly trusting to thee the germ will be blessed.

Ye great and exalted, when you tread the sweet leas,
Do you look with contempt on such pleasures as these?
The worldling may boast of his treasures of gold;
But more real pleasure such scenes they unfold.
The merchant may glory in his ships on the main,
May boast of the riches his storehouses contain.
The demagogue may strive, with promises alluring,
A good place for himself and the dear people securing.
The lawyer may devise fables his clients to please,
Caring naught for the truth, so he pockets his fees.

But give me the joy that the farmer's life brings,
The pleasures and treasures that from such a lot springs,—
To furrow the sod in the freshness of morn,
To see beauty unfolding in the green growing corn;
To hear the chatting of catbird on the blossoming bough,
Whilst following with blithe heart behind the brave plough;
To delve, O Mother Earth, in thy bosom generous and kind,
With heart responsive to thine, by Nature refined.

O'er the fruit-garden we'll now look, if you please,
And see the care which my friend bestows on his trees.
Here's the quince and the pear, both the standard and dwarf,
Secured by yon hedge from the winds of the north.
There's the peach, the cherry, and the apricot, too;
The nectarine, the plum, both the yellow and blue.
On each tree in the garden is a calabash hung:
There the old birds have nested and brought forth their
        young.
Thus cared for, they sing with their hearts full of glee,
Destroying the insect, thus protecting the tree.
In safety they wing o'er the fruit-embowered grove,
In rapture so winning they chant of their love.
Oft, beauteous songsters, you've delighted my eye
Whilst teaching your fledglings their first lessons to fly,

As, fluttering on short flights, coaxing the untried wing,
With your chirping and chattering you've made the grove
    ring.
Blessings on thee, blithe songster, blessed gift unto Man,
Much-loved present of heaven, unfolding God's plan.
Thou mind'st me of Paradise and the cherubim's wing,
As with praise and thanksgiving, gentle birdling, you sing.
And when you wander forth, oh! return hither again,
Return to these groves and rehearse your sweet strain.
For again, fairest warbler, I'd hear thee prolong
The song thou just sung, that soul-cheering song.
Gentle solace it had, sweet bird, for my breast,
For ofttime indeed has thy presence been blest.
Oh, then, hither return and again build thy nest.
Here in these bowers thou shalt in safety remain,
Here Cruelty's hand shall ne'er plan thy bane.
Hide, hide behind thee thy weapon! Taint, taint not the
    air,
And pollute not with thy presence this garden so fair.
Shame, shame on thee, fowler! Shame, shame on thy art!
Blush, blush for thy manhood! Oh, call it not sport,
And hasten that day when the law shall protect,
When the people shall rise and shall justly inflict
On these destroyers of robins and birds winged with blue,
And shall penalty inflict as the punishment due;
When the farmer his interest shall justly consider,
And secure his best friends from the prowling marauder;
When lawns, groves, and woodlands shall mourn never-
    more,
And the oriole swing safely in the tall sycamore;
When again shall be heard poor whip-poor-will's note,
When the song shall resound from the swamp-robin's throat,
When the dove shall wing safely on her errand of love,
And the woodcock may nestle by side of the cove.
Oh, hasten that day when the tiller of soil
Shall wilfulness restrain and idleness foil!

When, as of yore, the pheasant's drum shall resound,
And the coroneted woodpecker re-echo the sound;
When the blackbird shall build in the evergreen's crest,
And ungrudgingly take whate'er he loves best,—
Perchance 'tis a grain. But cast up the accounts,
And list as the sable-plumed warrior recounts,
As he vauntingly tells whilst upward he mounts,
How oft he has swooped on the grub in the corn,
How myriads of insects he has unpityingly torn.
Remember, O Farmer, the good he has done,
And return to the rafter that cherished old gun.

And, O Husbandman, spare that bush by the rill,
That clump in the meadow, that cedar on the hill,
That the birds o'er thy land a shelter may find.
Thus, Yeoman, use, use thy reason, act not as one blind,
But plant the hedge by the wayside : thou shalt reap thy re-
    ward.
From the grub and the wire-worm the birdling will guard ;
He will sing on the bough and protect thy young trees,
Whilst thou reap'st the wheat or enjoys't thy ease.
While thou sleep'st at morn or nap'st at noon,
The robin will thank thee with his blithe, merry tune ;
He will tap at thy window, and perch at thy shed,
Will bless thee from 'neath his bosom of red.

But if thou fail'st thus to care for thy friends,
Thou shalt reap a sore harvest, shall reap the whirlwinds !
In thy orchard the borer shall unmolestedly root,
And the caterpillar prey on the tender young shoot ;
The grasshopper will hatch and lead forth her brood,
While thy oxen shall low in vain for their food.
Thou shalt want bread for thy household, and grass for thy
    kine ;
Plagues as of Egypt shall, Farmer, be thine
If thou leav'st the songster uncared for to pine !

To yonder right in profusion is seen
Vegetables and flowers, cabbage, lettuce, and bean.
The small fruits, as the raspberry and strawberry rare,
These my friend has selected and cultured with care.
And here are the herbs,—balm, sage, and thyme.
Again, city friend, thou smil'st at my rhyme.

But criticise not too closely, thus quiet my fears,
And a prescription I'll give thee,—'twill lengthen thy years.
'Tis this: Take frequent draughts of chamomile tea,—
'Twill help thy pale face, and from headache 'twill free.
For the heartache, ofttimes with Nature commune;
List to her, to her melodious, harmonical tune.
Oft roam with her in the green, grassy lanes,
In the garden, the grotto, the groves, and the plains;
Thy soul she will quicken with her inspiring mood
As thou wander'st with her in loved solitude.
By the side of the rivulet that flows in the meadow,
As thou standest on the brink, 'neath the willow-tree's shadow,
List to waters as o'er the tiny cataract they tumble:
Music thou wilt hear midst the foam and the rumble.
Look all around thee: thou wilt everywhere find
That Nature has music to the well-attuned mind.
Gaze o'erhead, and with list'ning ear
Hear the grand cadence, melodious and clear.
Unstop thy deaf senses; thy soul shall awaken,
Thy light shall arise.   Thou art not forsaken!

Observe thou the planets, as they harmoniously roll.
For thee they were made,—mayhap the home of thy soul.
Walk forth in the forest, and 'neath the wide-spreading shade
See the beauty that decks the leaves as they fade.

Seek the sweet-scented lily; it neither toils nor it spins.
Quaff its delicate fragrance, 'twill ease thy heart-pains.

List to the tame bee and mark her swift flight ;
Follow her to her cell,—not her happiness to blight,
But to witness her felicity in the thickly-settled hive,—
See the concert of effort, how the community thrive.
These lessons of Nature, not in vain were they sent ;
True happiness learn, O Man : 'tis content.

x.

Walk forth, says my friend, ere the sun has arisen.
See the purple and gold that spans the horizon ;
See the plumage of birds and the beauty of form
In the dewdrop that bathes the face of the morn.
See the blossoms of spring and the glory of autumn.
Ah, if men would but look to what Wisdom has taught them,
Would but yield unto her implicit submission,
Thus their destiny fulfilling, their glorious mission !

And on this theme—the mission of Man—
My friend has his formula of Infinitude's plan.
Says he, God in His goodness never designed
But happiness and increase to the imperishable mind.
He points to that great bond of unfathomable love
Which encircles us round, from below and above.
That, tho' different from matter, from animals dissimilar,
Unlike the planets, the Pleiades, or e'en distant star,
Which are governed by instinct or laws that are fixed,
That man's condition is twofold, 'tis varied, 'tis mixed.
To the body of Nature his physique is allied ;
Automatic herein varied wants are supplied.
But his Consciousness 'tis free, and before him are set
Two roads, which, tho' forked, yet in the end meet.
That Man's like the fabled companion of Ulysses,— .
Can be changed if he listens to the voice of the Circes.
Like Eurylochus, be changed from the man to the brute ;
Or as Arion, who was saved by the sweet notes of his lute,

Which had charms that allured e'en the Dolphin's ear,
And brought them together at the vessel's side near.
E'en so is that music which in sweet numbers flow,
Which breathes in man's soul with cadence gentle and low,
Charming the lion, the tiger, the wolf, and the bear,
That a little child may lead them with no thought of fear.
The affections (says he) are as seraphim's note,
Which Reason should learn, should learn as by rote.
Thus man can be ONE, and true harmony find
In tranquillity, peace, and calmness of mind.
In youth, says my friend, should these be combined,
For the mind of the child 'tis as blank sheet of paper,
And childhood the time for culture and labor.
The heart is then plastic as clay to the potter,
The mother the tutor, with God to inspire her.
This the clue which will unravel the thread,—
This through the Cretan labyrinth Ariadne led,—
The affections! they're the hope of our race;
What is written by them time can ne'er efface.
Says my friend, 'tis the first years of childhood,
The first ten, that influence most for ill or for good;
These bias the greatest in Man's education,
For weal or for woe in life's preparation.
Hence, says he, the great need of Home,
Where the thoughts of the wanderer ever may roam,—
Of childhood's sweet home, the scene of joy and of bliss;
Of a father's loved councils, a mother's caress,—
An oasis in the desert. Such memories they smile;
They dawn from afar and from evil beguile,
Throw their loved shadows the vale of life o'er,
Illuming the soul on Faith's distant shore;
Whilst the mind 'tis enraptured with Home's much-loved
    scene,
With its pleasures and treasures unalloyed and serene.
Where these bind the heart with their amaranthine chain,
'Tis as consolation in grief and as solace in pain,—

'Tis as fountain at foot of Helicon's mount ;
But ne'er to Muse or Apollo is consecrated that fount,
That pure fountain of feeling which perennial flows.
O sweet source of bliss, loved soother in all our woes !
In thy balmy dews the wanderer may lave,
And find that blessed healing thy waters erst gave.

XI.

But let us away from grove, grotto, and stream ;
Let us enter the Home, let that be our theme.
Let us cease the philosophic, the moralizing strain,
And sing of sweet Home, free from sorrow and pain.
For a more happy sight ne'er to mortals is given
Than a well-ordered Home,—'tis a foretaste of heaven !
The sire, the head of this Home, is by culture refined,
Hospitable, warm, sincere, yet firm is his mind.
His dwelling, tho' spacious, yet no grandeur displays;
'Twas here his father before him ended his days.
My friend is not rich in lands or in funds,—
A few thousands at interest, a few hundred in bonds,
These, with his farm,—just seventy acres,—comprise his es-
    tate.
Riches greater than these he ne'er strove to create,
And labored not for mere pelf, for treasures of gold,—
'Twas not the bent of his mind, 'twas ne'er cast in that
    mould.
In years of his life, just threescore and ten,'
Opportunity was not wanting ; but ne'er would he listen
To the voice of the Siren, who promised great wealth
To be suddenly amassed, without labor or tilth.
To the voice of the temptress he turned a deaf ear,
Howe'er plausible her story, or specious she'd appear;
For many barks had he seen on Life's ocean bereft
Of mast, sail, and anchor, on the wild wave adrift.
They'd sailed forth in the morn full of gladness and glee,
But ere eve were a wreck on Speculation's deep sea.

Oft he said all true wealth must come from the earth,
That honor and virtue 'tis the mind's greatest worth,
That content is the secret, happiness the prize,
And heaven the goal toward which we should rise.
These he strove to inculcate by example and precept,
These the lessons he taught, in this pathway he kept.

And his children around him grew, an honor and stay,
A hope and a blessing, as his days ebbed away.
We'll glance at his home.   He's two sons and a daughter ;
She's single as yet,—tho' many have sought her,—
And all language 'tis feeble, and faltering my verse,
As her graces I type and her virtues rehearse.
Sweet Ellen ! in Memory's niche thou art placed.
In form she was perfected and draped with taste,
Her cheek slightly kissed by the sun's golden ray,—
The rose and the lily both sought for display.
The brown, 'twas the sun's and the soft summer's air ;
They'd printed their trace on brow and bosom as fair
As poet's maiden Lenore, radiant and rare.
In her sweet face health's roses beamed,
And in the blue of her eye intelligence gleamed ;
'Neath a sun-bonnet of blue stole a bright golden curl.
Ne'er of daughter was prouder a duke or an earl
Than my old friend, as he watched her so merrily tripping,
With her little niece by the hand, from the dairy-house skip-
        ping ;
For Ellen had a care besides her flowers and the household.
A brother was missing, a loved son, from the fold ;
The dread Archer had levelled, unerringly aimed,
And the uncertainty of life o'er the household proclaimed.
Of father and mother by one fell blow bereft,
And to Ellen's nurture and care a darling child left.

Oh, oft have I looked, sweet childhood, on thee,
As thou skip'st o'er the green, light-hearted and free ;

Oft gazed in thy eyes of unfathomable blue,
Noting each emotion, tender and true.
There's deep meaning in thy soft loving eyes,
Denoting each feeling,—now wonder, now surprise ;
E'en thy wilfulness but enhances thy grace
As each shadow is cast on thy sweet tiny face.
Oft thy dimpled cheek to my bosom I've pressed,
And round my neck I've received thy tender caress.
The rose it is sweet, the lily 'tis fair,
But the rose or the lily they ne'er can compare,
Loved babe, to thy brow, to thy bosom of snow.
In innocence, sweet gem, erst mayst thou grow !
May adverse winds waft over thee lightly,
And the season of youth pass over thee brightly !

'Tis eve : little Bess is seated on her grandfather's knee,
With both hands in his pockets, after the knife or the key.
There he playfully sits, much amused by her prattle,
In his usual place (after tea) on the old oaken settle,
Telling some simple story which her hands have beguiled
From his pockets.   'Tis ever thus with the child !
She's forgotten the spectacles, the knife, and the key,
And is now laughing and clapping, with her heart full of glee,
Over the oft-told theme about " Mother Hubbard,"
Or that other old lady with no bread in her cupboard.
Bess has heard this related ofttimes before.
She's ne'er satisfied yet : " More stories, grandfather, more."
He varies somewhat, 'tis now of the " Little Old Man,"
Or "Shove it in the oven as fast as you can."

O Childhood ! sweet Childhood, blessed condition,
Thou little miniature lass, sweet maidenhood's scion,
May thy pathway in life be strewed o'er with flowers, ˙
Thus thy childhood be passed 'midst Affection's fair bowers !

But hark ! 'twas a knock ; 'tis caught Ellen's quick ear.
John opens the door ; a manly form doth appear,

His face all aglow as he salutes his old friends,
Shakes hands with them all.   Toward Ellen he bends,
A greeting confused 'twixt rudeness and shame.
With a glow on his cheek, he scarce mentions her name,
But is soon chatting with her brothers about the state of the
          weather, —
About the time there has been—yes, weeks altogether—
That the heavens seemed sealed, the earth all aglow.
The pastures are parched ; oh, that the torrents would flow !
That the farmers (quoth Ben) the golden wheat could be
          sowing ;
For neighbor Smith says ne'er a grain will be growing,
That while the soil is thus parched 'tis folly to furrow.
This, says he, they who try it will find to their sorrow :
That the germ 'twill sprout and then wither away.
So till it rains, says he, let the seed lay.
Would it not be better, father, that we also delay?

Nay, my son, delay not ; 'tis the sluggards' excuse,
Who lavish on Nature without stint their abuse.
Nothing can suit them ; they keep a perpetual outcry,—
The seasons ! the weather ! 'tis too wet, cold, or dry !
To these perpetual grumblers there's nothing aright ; .
In the spring 'tis the fly, in the summer the blight.
Now, my son, this drought 'tis doubtless designed
For a purpose that's good by the Infinite mind.
'Tis by this means the earth a respite obtains
From the exhaustion that's caused by too frequent rains,
And particles of nourishment in the subsoil below
To the surface, by absorption, with facility will flow.
Thus Providence adapts, Nature seeks to comply,
And the medium 'tis established 'twixt waste and supply.
Depend on it, my son, Nature ne'er is uncertain ;
Her laws are self-acting, never fruitless or vain.
And tho' Man's finite reason can ne'er comprehend,
Yet God has in all things shaped the means to the end.

The heat of the summer, the bleak winds of spring,
All have their purpose, each blessings bring.
Is it not, then, great presumption and folly in Man
Thus, captious, to cavil at Infinitude's plan ?
For law is prescribed to matter and space,
Each world in its orbit, each star in its place ;
The mist, the sea, the clouds, and the earth
Are all pre-evolved in Nature's sure birth.
With her grandfather's voice Bess's here blended ;
The lecture 'twas shortened, the contention 'twas ended.
For a baby so well bred, certainly 'twas rude
To dissent thus so pointed from what she ne'er understood.
Grandfather soothed, he reasoned, he smiled,
And though the temper Bessie displayed 'twas neither gentle
      nor mild,
Yet 'twas not in his heart to thwart the dear orphaned child.
Nonplussed was his philosophy, 'twas confounded, 'twas foiled,
Subdued and o'ercome by a child that'd been spoiled.
Her rights she asserted, the gauntlet threw down,
Unappeased by a promise, unawed by a frown.
She was weary and sleepy and wanted her bed, ·
Was tired of dry talk, thus snapped the argument's thread.
Her grandfather soothed, and soon with flying feet
The angel came and lull'd to visions sweet.
O Sleep ! gentle, balmy, dewy Sleep !
As o'er our wearied senses thy numbing opiates creep,
With healing, sweet healing on their wing,
And o'er Thought's temple their rich curtains fling,
With downy softness on each fold replete.
And tho' Life and Death in shadows meet,
And steep in wondrous and mysterious dreams,
And tho' dead to thought, yet sensation gleams,
And o'erflowing fills with magic light
The mind's cathedral, and fancies bright
Pour forth with dazzling beam,
And things are not what they seem.

Loved art thou, O Sleep, in youth or in age ;
All joys thou increaseth and all sorrows assuage.
All, all know thy gentle, thy loving embrace.
Yes, thy blessings are unnumbered, impartial thy grace.

While Bessie was cradled at her grandfather's side,
Edward and Ellen, on Love's buoyant tide,
Walked o'er the garden, and 'neath the moon's silver ray.
Silent they paced, while the youth made essay
To speak of the thought he'd resolved on that day,
Which he'd resolved on before; but his tongue disobeyed
The impulse of thought.   Tho' bold, he was afraid.
Love made him a coward, and ne'er could he tell
For the force of the torrent that gushed in the well ;
But his intent was now fixed,—he'd broke through the spell
That enthralled, had conn'd in his mind a love-lit oration,
In reply to which depended, he thought, his salvation.
'Twas this so abashed him when he entered the door
That he scarce knew e'en he stood on his head or the floor.
The hour had arrived ; he breathed short and fleet.
The heart in his bosom loud, loud did it beat.

*   *   *   *   *   *   *   *

XII.

The birds no longer thrill the vernal grove,
No longer loudly tell their faithful love ;
But stilled is note of robin, sparrow, and the dove.
Above, beneath, around, unnumbered fire-flies flit,
And o'er the garden silently their magic light emit.   .
The bat, as if rejoicing in the soft and balmy air,
Rejoicing that the hour had come to quit his daily lair,
He lingered round the arbor, as if list'ning there.
Oh, blessed hour of eve !   Enchantment reigns,
And balmy dews refresh the sultry plains.
The placid light of moon is on the wane,
And, lo ! 'tis Venus with her vestal train.

On her the lovers gaze, enraptured gaze,
And silent watch her quiet, mystic ways.
Edward, if through fear he'd been remiss,
Has told his Hope, and all, all is bliss.

O Love, when thou art pure as that in Edward's breast,
Upgushing from the heart and by the soul expressed,
Thy possessor is of fortune, of fortune rare possesst.
Poor he may be, yet ne'er in Golconda's mine
Are richer rubies, none more brilliant shine
Than Love's jewels, reset at Hymen's shrine.

Years have fled since within that garden's pale
Edward unto Ellen breathed the tender tale,
Years have passed, and now, in cot, in green'st vale,
Love has blossomed, and, lo! a full-blown rose
Has bloomed.   There in those glades doth wedded love repose,
Secluded there, sequestered from life's busy, bustling crowd,
Hid from the curious, prying eye, hid from the vain and proud.
There oft beside the social, cheerful, friendly fire,
There much I love to chat, at times I oft retire,
And witness Hymen's guileless, undivided joys,
See smiling Industry that each passing hour employs,
As bee, in culling bliss from fairest, sweetest flowers.
Yes, in that vale there blooms Houstonian bowers.
Nightshade 'tis not cultured, nor oleander grows,
Nor envy, nor ambition clog the current as it flows ;
But, peacefully meandering on the tranquil stream of Life,
No deaf'ning cataract's roar allures to scenes of strife.
Ne'er has city's din one charm for Edward's eye,
Nor luxury's pomp e'er caused in Ellen's breast a sigh.
Pledges, three pledges from the treasury of heaven,
Three blessed gifts, these, these have been given.
Ellen has known a mother's joy, a mother's care and bliss,
And Edward felt at eve a cherub's loving kiss.
Yes, little prattlers run " to lisp their sire's return,"
And Love in that Home its altars brightly burn.

THE OLD SENATE CHAMBER.

LINES WRITTEN ON THE OCCASION OF A VISIT TO WASH-
INGTON IN 1860.

I.

WITHIN these walls have sounded
    Thoughts, immortal thoughts, which will survive
The mottled-marble columns, firmly grounded
    On their base, which, protecting, give
Their massive strength to uphold a dome
    Grander than the Ephesian reared,
Or that which graced the Capitol at Rome
    In palmy days, when she appeared
As mistress, ruling by the sceptre and the rod
The nations round, who trembled at her nod.

II.

Massive ruins still evince and prove
    The Coliseum's glory, the Pantheon's pride.
O'er Rome, Athens, Carthage we may rove,
    They all attest to Time's unceasing tide,—
Rolling on, relentless in its sway,
    Engulfing the proudest monuments of art,
And sweeping with the besom of decay
    Into the tomb, smiting with Death's dart
Alike Man, his science and his skill,
Before Time's unpitying, relentless will.

46

III.

The hand and mind of Man have reared
  In ancient times and Science smiled
O'er mighty trophies, which have appeared
  In grandeur 'midst the desert wild,
And yet e'en now exist in Egypt's sand.
Art, with its magic-working wand,
Has reared with Sculpture's cunning hand,
  And Glory crowned the classic land
Of Italy with wreaths by Fancy spun,—
Wreaths which Petrarch and Dante won.

IV.

But thou, our country's Capitol, to thee!
  Where fair Freedom with her altars new,
Alone now standing, baptized to Liberty
  By sacred recollections not a few.
And as the eaglet on the snow-clad height
  Peers proudly from the mountain's crest,
So waves Columbia's banner, girt with light,
  A star of Freedom, gleaming in the West,
Borne on the breeze, floating o'er the sea,
The emblem of Union, the flag of the free!

V.

O'er the Capitol floats that starry banner.
  Long may it wave, Columbia's thine!
'Tis the patriot's hope, the patriot's prayer.
  Long may the stars of Freedom shine!
And though beneath the waves of high debate,
  As the Atlantic's, surging meet and fall,
And thoughts pregnant with an empire's fate
  Echo through the Senate Hall,—
Speech eloquent, majestic, stately, grand,
Conveyed by wings of lightning o'er the land.

VI.

O Eloquence! majestic is thy art,
  And wondrous is thy skill to move.
Thou hast a spell to dull the heart
  With hate or woo the soul to love ;
And now as when the Athenian thundered,
  Or when Paul declared the Word,
And Felix saw and tremblingly wondered·
  (Though to his convenience he still deferred).
Yet Paul the Light of Life unsealed,
And Felix felt that Power revealed.

VII.

Pause ! thy step is now on classic ground.
  Within this hall the clarion voice of Clay
Has pealed and sounded round
  The walls.   Oft in the stirring affray
I've watched that gallant chieftain's plume,—
  Thou wast my first, my youthful choice.
But now, alas ! within the silent tomb,
  By Death is stilled thy magic voice.
No more its silver tones will roll
O'er the land, to move and thrill the soul.

VIII.

Illustrious man ! patriot, orator, and sage,
  Thy memory 'tis entombed in the hearts
Of thy countrymen, and History's living page
  Will tell thy nature's wondrous art
To move and magnetize the soul,
  Thy power, utterance, and marvellous speech,
That moved thy hearers and controlled
  The multitude within thy reach.
Thou art gone! not forgotten, but endeared
To thousands, loved, honored, and revered.

IX.

And here, too, thy inimitable compeer,
  Senator from the land of flowers,
Inflexible, sedate, severe, austere,
  As scornfully above all deceit he towers,
Smiting with weapon keen and bright
  As Saladin's sabre.   With no weak arm
He battled for what he deemed the right,
  Fearless and regardless of the harm.
'Twas seen and felt, in his career,
His dread ideal he pursued unmoved by fear.

X.

And he, our charter's great defender,
  He whom New England loved so well,
Columbia's sons shall tribute render
  And his mighty prowess tell.
He went not forth to the battle of debate
  On small occasions, but when he'd tax
His mighty energies he was wondrous great.
  Like Cœur de Leon, wielded he the battle-axe
With might.   Yes, his opponent reeled
'Neath blows that levelled lance and shield.

XI.

Thy sun has set, but thou hast left behind
  Enough for mortal man to leave.
The enduring products of thy gigantic mind
  Are deathless, and shall ever live
Whilst man shall speak in Shakespeare's tongue,
  Whilst shines in beauty Freedom's sun.
Whilst Milton's graphic verses shall be sung,
  Or laurel wreaths by Genius won,
Shall Freedom praise thy mighty aid,
And Eloquence repose beneath thy shade.

5

XII.

Illustrious triumvirate, wondrous three !—
    America, they were types of thine ;
Unsubdued and undaunted, gallant and free,
    Firm and erect as the evergreen pine !—
Your dust now guarded by your native mountains,
    Entombed beneath Columbia's soil,
Watered by the gurgling fountains
    In the land for which you toiled,
In the hearts of millions cherished,
Your virtues live, your faults have perished.

XIII.

There, not distant from the Speaker's chair,
    There Benton sat, the lion-hearted,
With independent mien and kingly air,
    With mind unfettered and undaunted.
Did Faction seek to bind his soul
    With shackles, or with " Democratic rules"
To fetter his conscience or control
    His reason ?   He scorned the tools
Of Presidents.   Dire Faction ne'er could tame,
Nor Party e'er obscure his honor or his fame.

XIV.

Old Hall ! thy walls have ofttimes echoed
    With thought and word now told by pen,
By art inscribed, by type and ode,
    The genius of those mighty men,—
Wright, Clayton, Webster, Benton, Clay,
    Calhoun, Linn, Macon, and the rest.
All, all have gently passed away,
    All, all have bowed to Death's behest.
Ye rulers who direct the helm of state,
Those patriots' zeal for country imitate ;
Shun, shun their faults, their virtues emulate.

WILLIAM PENN'S HOLY EXPERIMENT.

READ AT THE ANNIVERSARY OF THE BI-CENTENNIAL OF
ABINGTON MONTHLY MEETING, ON FIRST DAY, TWELFTH
MONTH 3, 1882.*

PART I.

'MIDST the sylvan scenes of England,
  As the autumn's sun shone down,
Struggling thro' the misty vapors
  Settled densely 'round the town,
Settled o'er the spire and steeple,
  O'er the sweetly-scented leas,
Faintly beams the morning sun,
  Gently wafts the ocean breeze.
Higher in his flight ascending,
  Onward with a monarch's sway,
Upward on his mission wending,
  Melting mist with glowing ray.

---

* The records of Abington Monthly Meeting date its origin back to the
meeting held at Shackamaxon on the 8th of Ninth month, 1682, which ante-
dates the arrival of William Penn. That meeting was held in part "in order,"
it is stated, " to appoint other meetings where it may be thought best to meet."
After the arrival of Penn, our Monthly Meeting was not merged into the
Philadelphia Meeting, as some seem to think ; but, as our books show, Thomas
Fairman, when he removed to Tacony, " at the Governor's request, provided
a book for the service of the meeting." Different books there may have been,
for in 1719 George Boon was directed to procure the one now in our posses-
sion, transcribing the proceedings therein from former records.

'Twas on a peaceful Sabbath morn,
  In a quaint old English town,
Thus baptized in vapors dense
  As the slanting rays came down.
Nowhere but 'neath England's skies
  Do such scenes the eye delight,
Nowhere beams the sun's bright rays
  With such subdued and mellowed light.
In her noiseless, tranquil way,
  Nature to the soul reveal'd,
And on that quiet Sabbath-day
  To the heart and mind appeal'd.

Beyond the village quaint and old,
  There, beneath an oak-tree's shade,
There a straw-roof'd cot was reared,—
  In ancient times such cots were made ;
Woodbines old adorned the walls,
  Roses clustered round the door,
Age and moss o'erlaid the floor,
  Laid with tiles in time of yore.

Ope the door and walk within.
  There are maid and matron fair,
Waiting for the gift divine ;   .
  Adjusted every earthly care,
In stillness thus endowed,
  There in quietude engaged.
Seated there in tranquil calm
  Upon those benches quaint and aged,
There is manhood crowning prime,
  There are locks with age all white,
There is youth's sweet budding time,
  Waiting for the heavenly light.

From the altar of each soul
Ascends the heartfelt prayer ;
The solemn mien, the holy calm
Attested God was there.

After stillness for a time
The silence now was broken,
And words of cheer with gospel power
By William Penn were spoken.
Inspired with Christian grace and truth,
With wisdom from above,
Touched with tenderest sympathy
From Fountain source of love,
As with live coal from off the altar,
Teaching love for man, our brother.
Tho' in life he oft may falter,
Still love ye always one another.

Thus the speaker earnest spoke,
Spoke of Christ, the light within,
Vouchsafed to all mankind,
Redeeming every soul from sin
Who loves the heavenly Child,*
Who listens and obeys His voice,
Which leads in virtue's narrow path,
Making every soul rejoice
In the glorious victory won !
Resist not, then, the heavenly vision,
But onward in the rugged path,
The path pursued to land Elysian !

---

* The Society of Friends have been much *misunderstood* in consequence of the *stress* which they have ever placed upon the doctrine and *fact* of " regeneration." Upon this subject they agree with Martin Luther, who says, " Every Christian may enjoy this birth of Christ not less than if he also, like Jesus, were born bodily of the Virgin Mary. Whoso disbelieves or doubts this," he says, " is no Christian." ·

That promised land within thee lies,
  Look thou to guide within :
The way that leads to Paradise
  Is conquest over sin.

The preacher paused, as burst the door,
  As armed men filled the rustic hall.
"Seize, seize the rogues !" the captain cried.
  "Man and women, seize them all !
Stop that prating fellow's mouth,
  The babbler vile, the uncouth boor,
Who speaks against our church and state !
  Let him o'er the tread-mill tour.
Cease your clack, you vile blasphemer !
  What have you done indeed ?
A pretty question that to ask.
  For law and justice you would plead ?
Leisure plenty you shall have,
  Full twelve months or so,
To study England's glorious code,—
  To Newgate, ranter, you shall go !"

Amidst malefactors vile
  Was thus unjustly placed
One of England's greatest sons
  That e'er her annals graced.

Again o'er England's sea-girt isle
  Shone the sun's dim light,
Glanced a moment o'er the land,
  Then vanished from the sight.
The clouds assumed a threat'ning hue,
  From Isle of Wight to Irish Sea,
And Nature seemed herself incensed
  At England's deep iniquity.

From Dover's Strait to Solway's Forth
    Roared Heaven's aerial guns,
From Plymouth's Sound to farthest North
    The torrents poured in tuns.
Oaks which had centuries bravely stood,
    Their time had come at last,
Loosed in the tempest's fearful roar,
    Seared by the lightning's blast.

If on the land the Storm Spirit raged
    With a fierce, convulsive motion,
Terrific was the mighty force
    With which he stirred the ocean.
You that dwell 'midst flocks and herds,
    That dwell in the earth's content,
Ah, little ye know the mighty power
    With which the wild waves rent.
Old Neptune spoke in every surge
    That lashed Old England's shore ;
The lightning leaped from cliff to cliff
    To join the dreadful roar.
Two hundred sail cleft ocean's wave,*—
    Thus English annals tell,—
The waves closed o'er those hearts so brave
    And tolled their funeral knell.

Nature again serenely smiled,
    The skies were clad with tints of blue ;
With gentle glance the sun shone down,
    With beams so kindly true.
'Tis thus with Nature, thus with Man :
    The earthquake's shock, quick 'tis o'er ;
Vehement passions soon react,
    And smiles succeed the tempest's roar.

---

* A historical fact.

PART II.

The sheriff brought his prisoner forth,
  The jury was impanelled and arrayed,
And in the form of English law
  The clerk the indictment read.
" Prisoner, stand forth !   Is your name Penn ?"
  Inquired the judge, with features stern.

" Since thus my lot in life hath changed,"
  Said Penn, with manner firm,
" It hath thy memory much deranged."

" I know you not, nor do I wish to know
  Such as you, that grovel in the earth.
Your father, Admiral Penn, right well, I know,
  Did rue the day that gave you birth.
You dishonored and disgraced his name,—
  Your father's name, a name of worth,—
And seek to tarnish England's fame,
  The land that gave you birth."

" Who constituted thou both judge
  And counsel 'gainst the accused ?
I call upon the jury, who are my peers,
  To be not from the right seduced.
My cause is the cause of every Englishman ;
  Your cause, whate'er your creed !
I affirm to you, my countrymen,
  That I am innocent, in word, in deed,
In intention, act, or utterance.
  I am utterly incapable of doing aught
That would our English name disgrace ;
  Not so much as by the slightest thought
Would I upon it bring dishonor or reproach.
  It cannot be that it offends

The majesty of our laws to worship God !
　For this I sought to meet my friends,
Assembling orderly, peacefully, sedately,
　Nor in the least degree tumultuously,
As in that false indictment charged ;
　But decently, soberly, not seditiously,
We assembled, and with grateful hearts
　Sincerely offered thanks to heaven
For the many gifts, unmerited, conferred,
　For the blessings daily, hourly given.''

"Sirrah !" said the judge, with angry tone,
　"You shall not be permitted thus to plead,
With cunning tongue and utterance false,
　The jury seeking to mislead.
'Tis not for worshipping God you're tried,
　But for wandering without the bounds
Which law and custom hath ordained.
　In company with unmannered clowns,
You seek to gain some notoriety.
　For shame ! a man of your estate
To set such vile example,—
　To cast discredit on the church and state !''

" I affirm that I have no law broken.
　'Tis as clear a case of tyranny
As e'er disgraced our native land,
　Of persecution and of bigotry.
And I firmly stand upon my rights,
　As secured in our great charter ;
Nor will I yield them up to might,
　Tho' I may suffer as a martyr
In the cause of truth and right.
　My countrymen, in times of yore
Our fathers suffered much for conscience ;
　Many were the persecutions sore they bore

From tyrant, from papist, and from pope.
　　Again, I fear, our eyes may gaze,
And history mark another page,
　　As in those fearful, bloody days.
Let Persecution have her horrid sway,
　　Make it a crime to speak and think,
Then Bigotry will rule this land,
　　And all our rights in darkness sink,
Our families ruined and our children 'slaved.
　　Base-born informers in the light of day
Will gladly revel in ill-gotten gains ;
　　Our rights would vanish, be explained away,
And Justice seek more congenial skies.
　　Superstition will the land control,
New schemes invent, old tortures ply,
　　Thought to fetter and to bind the soul,
To stifle Freedom in her island home !
　　'Seeking to erase from English hearts
By means imported o'er the seas—
　　By crafty stealth, by priestly arts—
Our nation's glory, our island's boast !
　　The Inquisition, as in times of yore,
Will rear its blood-stained crest,
　　And Britain's sons will bleed at every pore.
O ! from the land such noxious weeds efface.
　　Let toleration, like the orb of day,
Irradiate each heart and glow in every face,
　　Illuming with its bright protecting ray
The heaths and homes of native land.
　　Such day will dawn ; I see it breaking !
I see intolerance, with her hideous band,
　　Shame-faced, our shores forsaking.''

　　" 'Tis said the pen is mighty,'' quoth the judge,
　　" But your tongue, fellow, hath no end.

Tho' 'gainst you I have no grudge,
  Yet by your discourse you so rend
And pervert the truth by falsehood
  That you our patience doth exhaust.
  Your remarks most plainly show
  That to sense and reason you are lost,
And I charge and warn the jury
  Not to credit such vile fanaticism.
Rather let them look to England's good,—
  How the church is rent with schism,
How the laws by wild fanatics,
  By these ranting, canting heretics,
Are perverted and abused.
  See you teach such whining lunatics,
Preaching doctrines foolish and absurd,
  That the law hath yet a might,
And English juries some respect
  For order, custom, and for right !"

" Not guilty !" was the verdict rendered.
  And tho' the judge, with fierce invective,
Blustered, stormed, and threatened,
  Evincing malice vile, vindictive,
Still the jury firm remained,
  And, as verdict just and true,
" Not guilty !" they again returned,—
  Yes, thrice returned, as Freedom's due.
With no respect to this, howe'er,
  The judge bore down the right
And remanded Penn to prison,
  Thus crushing law with power and might,
Charging him with vile sedition,
  With contempt of judge and court,
With conniving at high treason.
  And with sarcastic mien and port,

Taunting spoke he of Penn's mission.
   " Sheriff !"—hear you the voice that calls?—
" Let him with Bunyan be companioned
   Within the stout old castle's walls."

PART III.

Flowing thus from mighty fountain,
   Has the truth rolled o'er
The ages that have passed away ;
   And flowing still with power,
With beauty, and with might,
   Gurgling, flowing from the mountains,
Now resistless in its course,
   Ever fed by unseen fountains,
As it beautifies the earth !
   Now it swells the throbbing tide
Of a swiftly flowing river,
   Rolling in its native pride.

Can ye bind that mighty torrent,
   Strive to check it at its source ?
Bind it down with bands of steel,
   Fetter it with might and force ?

Can the truth be thus subdued,
   Thus subdued its sweet perfume ?
No ! the more to earth 'tis crushed,
   The richer, sweeter is its bloom !

Let Superstition try her hand.
   Fetter it in dungeons dire,
Smother it with dread and fear ;
   Burn it in a martyr's fire,
Ply the torture, ply the screw ;
   Revive again Torquemanda's reign,
Ply that doubly damned invention
   In Religion's sacred name ;

Close the heart to human anguish,
  Demons seeking to affright ;
Call servile Ignorance to aid,—
  Hideous is his brutal might,
Ever Superstition's minion,—
  With his buckler and his shield,
Sturdiest champion of Opinion,
  Always last to quit the field ;
Let King Custom join your ranks,
  With his mighty, mighty legion,—
Reinforced your holy phalanx
  From your famous ally's region.

All in vain your legions battle,
  All in vain your forces fight,
All in vain your stupid cattle,
  Marshalled by their chosen knight.

'Gainst you is arrayed the Truth,
  Clad in radiant armor bright.
Lo ! the conquering legions come ;
  Error, darkness put to flight.

Methinks I see in visions bright,
  Shining thro' the mists of time,
Heroes clad in radiant light,
  Illuming every age and clime.

Methinks I see in Virtue's track
  The gathering storm, the tempest's wrath,
The cross, the scaffold, and the rack,
  The jeering taunt, the rugged path.

Methinks I see the path they trod,
  The course they took to heaven above,—
The pathway which leads up to God,
  The path bestrewed with deeds of love.

6

From o'er the centuries comes a voice,
  Resounding, pealing, loud and clear,
A voice that makes the heart rejoice,
  Sometimes distant, sometimes near.
From Calvary's Mount to native strand,
  In ancient or in modern times,
Ringing clear in fatherland,
  Breaks the air those gracious chimes.
From Him whom all our households cherish
  Sound those chimes, sweet and clear,—
" Truth shall never, never perish ;
  I am ever, ever near."

Sadly, sadly sound those chimes,
  Chanting o'er the honored dead ;
Chanting of historic times,
  They touch the heart, those requiems sad.

Mournfully, mournfully chants that tone,
  Chanting o'er earth's flowery breast,
Chanting o'er from zone to zone,
  Where'er those martyred heroes rest.

Joyfully, joyfully peal those chimes,
  Pealing forth each hero's name,
Joyfully sounding through all time,
  Sounding loud their deathless fame.

Gently, gently sweeps that lyre,
  Unseen, tuned by mystic hand ;
Vibrate those notes, our souls inspire,
  From the unseen heavenly land !*

---

* The sufferings of Friends in England, and also in New England, seem incredible from our present stand-point. After the Restoration, in 1680, it was estimated that two hundred and forty-three persons died in consequence of

PART IV.

'Twas midnight ; darkness as a shroud
   Hung o'er the land, hung o'er the seas,
And sleep, tired Nature's soothing balm
   From many a pang that Fate decrees,
Emancipating thought, and nerve and brain,
   From care, from sorrow, and from pain.
As Nature's opiate wrought its charm,
   And Labor rose refreshed again,
With mind elastic and with cheerful heart,
   With arm to strike and soul to will,
Its purpose high, and renew again its round,
   Its daily round, with pride and skill !

Behind the hills had set the orb of day,
   But within the palace walls light,
Life, and revelry held noisy sway,
   And song and laughter put to flight
All thoughts of trouble or of care ;
   Seductive, gentle music filled the air
With joyous and voluptuous notes,—
   The scene was wondrous, enchanting fair.

---

their hardships,—" having been so grievously beaten and wounded, because of their frequenting religious assemblies, that they died of their hurts and wounds." In New England they were, if possible, still more inhumanly used ; they were tortured, beaten, and hanged.

To narrate one instance, as given by Sewel : " Hored Gardner, an inhabitant of Newport, came with her sucking babe, and a girl to carry it, to Weymouth, from whence, for being a Quaker, she was hurried to Boston, where both she and the girl were whipped with a threefold knotted whip. After the whipping, the woman kneeled down and prayed the Lord to forgive those persecutors, which so reached a woman that stood by that she said, ' Surely she could not have done this if it had not been by the spirit of the Lord.' "

Beauty, with bright eye and rosy lip,
　　With lithesome foot and merry tongue,
And love forbidden and forbade,
　　Around the scene enchanted hung,
Stealing like a deceptive sprite,
　　With a magic and enticing smile,
Intoxicating with exhilarating draught
　　Its victims, and with crafty wile
Alluring to the broad, elastic river's side,—
　　If not to embark upon the fatal tide,
And float resistless on the deceitful stream,
　　Where barks unnumbered ride
And silken sails spread to the breeze.
　　With measured music gliding o'er
The water, amid the ripple and the spray,
　　No thought at first of that deceptive shore
On which many a gallant ship has stranded,
　　Beguiled from port by Pleasure's gales,
Enticed from anchorage safe and sure,
　　Allured by Hope to spread her sails,
And driving toward that fatal shore,—
　　Drifting hopeless, helpless in the storm,
By gales tempestuous borne along,
　　Life wrecked and Virtue's anchor gone !

England's monarch was seated
　　Not distant from this exultant throng,
Clad for the festival with pomp and pride ;
　　He who spoke with wisdom's tongue,
But often wrought with foolish deed,
　　Was with skill and care arrayed
To tread the paths which Pleasure trod.
　　"Speak out, be not afraid,"
The merry monarch sportive said ;
　　And as he spoke, with courtly bow,
Withdrew the covering from his head.

" Thou makest jest, Friend Charles,"'
  Replied the Quaker.
" Thou knowest that we Friends,
  Except in thanksgiving to our Maker,
Cannot, for conscience' sake,
  Uncover or bow to man the head.
We mean not to give offence,
  To appear ill-mannered or ill-bred ;
But think that empty compliments,
  So much the fashion of our day,
Savor much of gross hypocrisy,
  And lead the mind from God away."

" Nay, Friend William,
  We want no discourse to-night,"
Good-natured spoke the king,
  " Of faith or works or inner light.
Say quickly what you have to say,
  For we must soon be gone ;
Tho' with persuasion you might, perchance,
  Join in the merry, jovial throng !
In the hall above you hear
  The notes of love and joy,
The light, fantastic glee of youth,
  The peerless voice of maiden coy.
Join in the merry, festive scene,
  And be not thus estranged,—
Join, Friend William, join the dance !
  Ere you had your spleen deranged,
Whilst living 'neath the skies of France,
  You loved to join in Pleasure's maze,
To mingle in life's buoyant tide,—
  You loved our cheerful English ways.

" Nay, I forbid ! No discourse to-night
  That savors in the least of preaching.

In days gone by I'd quite enough,
 In Scotland's clime, of pious teaching.
So you're not satisfied, it seems,
 With prisons, buffetings, and blows
On England's merry, merry shores,
 But you need seek more savage foes
O'er ocean's stormy, boist'rous wave.
 Why surely, William, friend,
Those cannibals will eat you up,
 And limb from limb will rend
Your English carcasses, so round and sleek.
 Nay ! we'll not have it so indeed,
To let you thus such dangers face ;
 For, though it be against your creed,
We'll put you in the proper path.
 There can go as passengers
A regiment of Oliver's stout old troop.
 Take them, those evil messengers,
Lounging now the town about ;
 They'll pray and keep their powder dry,
They'll put your enemies to rout.
 Take them, their freight we'll pay,
For 'twill confer a favor to the State
 To send those rascals o'er the seas away,—
They also keep your top-knot on your pate.
 Take them, we wish you happiness and joy ;
'Twill thus confirm the saying trite—
 You know it—about the two birds and the boy.''

 '' Thou jesteth still,'' said Penn.
  '' Seriously, I implore thee, incline thy ear
And patiently listen to my request.
 My people are o'erborne with care,
With persecution and oppression sore,
 And we seek a home wherein to live

In safety, there to dwell in quietness and peace.
　　And we humbly pray thee, O king, to give
Thy sanction to our most reasonable request.
　　The State, as thou know'st, owed
My father sixty thousand crowns,
　　For services long since bestowed.
Give but thy grant in virgin soil,—
　　'Tis all I ask for that just claim,—
And suffer not thy mind to be misled,
　　Deceived by reasons impotent and lame."

" When we this audience granted,"
　　Said the king, " fixed was our mind ;
Naught since our thought has changed.
　　Fear not that aught behind
Can e'er the right or just o'erthrow,
　　For forthwith without delay our hand
Shall sign and seal the royal charter,
　　And to you and yours convey the land
For which you have petitioned,
　　With all the bounds and privileges assign'd.
So thus I hope, my faithful friend,
　　That we've relieved your mind."

PART V.

O'er the wild waves she sails gallantly on,
　　The billows in gladness they urge her along ;
Thro' the spray and the breakers she dashes away,
　　The zephyrs float 'round her in music and song.
The sunbeam in beauty walks over the deep,
　　Folding the vessel in halo so bright,
Streaming on pinion that floats on the breeze
　　O'er the fair ocean, that mirror of light.
Like a sea-bird she skims on the salt water's wave.
　　Aloft the sailor-boy whistles in freedom and glee ;

He thinks of his home on the far-distant shore,
　O'er the wide waters, across the deep sea.
She bears in her bosom naught of the sorrow of sin ;
　She bears in her bosom the hopes of the free,
Is loaded with treasures far richer than gold,—
　She is freighted with blessings, with fair liberty.
The goddess of freedom, the angel of peace,
　They guarded that vessel; they saw from afar
The germ that she carried, the wealth she conveyed.
　This they saw as light twinkles from yon distant star.

PART VI.

Drop the anchor, furl the sail!
　Ho! our sailing now is o'er.
See the pleasant, pleasant land,
　See the green, inviting shore!
God be thank'd for dangers past,
　God be blessed for joys to come!
Far behind is native land,
　Yonder is our future home!
See the skiffs with emblems peaceful,
　Each containing full a score
Of those tall and stalwart red men,
　Pushing out from yon green shore!

Now they cluster round the vessel,*
　Clad in Nature's tawny vest,
Waving high the green elm-branches,
　Shouting welcome to their guest.
All Nature echoes welcome! welcome!
　The waves that strike the vessel's side,

---

* William Penn says the air smelled as sweet as a garden in bloom. As they sailed up the river they received visits and invitations from the inhabitants.

Floating seaward in their course.
  Welcome! throbs the gurgling tide,
As the waters onward, onward glide.
  The warbling songsters of the grove
Prolong with sweetest strains,—
  They seem'd as envoys from above!
Not in Ark in time of flood
  Did message brought by beak of dove
Convey more joyous token.
  As theirs, our souls were filled with love;
No more their hearts rejoiced than ours,
  Just off the stormy ocean,
Where passed the dreary, dreary hours
  In one unvaried, changeless motion.
Joyous is the sight of land
  When off the stormy sea;
Joyous to the sea-bound heart
  Is then the flow'ry lea.
Joyful are the thoughts of home,
  Twinkling o'er the ocean far;
In every heart Home's ray of love
  Shines like a radiant star.
In the palace, in the cot,
  Universal glows that flame,
Proclaiming loud in Nature's voice,
  All o'er the world is man the same,
All o'er does love most potent reign.
  From burning sand to dreary waste,
It girts the earth with magic chain,
  From north to south, from east to west!

PART VII.

Beneath a broad, umbrageous elm
  Upon the gentle river's bank,
Seated in half-moon upon the ground,
  Grouped as they ranged in rank,

The chiefs were gravely circled round
    The great and generous Tammany,*
Who, above the rest, on grassy mound
    Was seated,—king of warriors free,
King elect by voice of braves,
    King chosen for his noble mind.
The squaws and younglings of the tribe
    In silent wonder sat behind.
The council-fire in front blazed bright,
    Friendship's emblem true and just,
For thus the red man lights the fire,—
    'Tis said to burn distrust.

With grave and thoughtful mien
    The strangers slow advance.
Before is Penn, with sash of blue,
    With kind and genial glance.

Tammany, with grace, extends his hand,
    And with eager, piercing ken
He met that frank and manly glance,
    In which sincerity was seen.
The warrior read with instinct true,
    Read with unerring Nature's eye,
As ray of light flits through the mist,
    As lightning flashes o'er the sky.

---

* Tammany was greatly venerated by the Indians, and though the whites canonized him St. Tammany, but little has been preserved concerning him. All we know, says Heckewelder, is that he was an ancient Delaware chief who never had his equal. His mark is affixed to a deed dated 23d day of Fourth month, 1683.

His name signifies "the affable," and he was greatly esteemed as a prophet-sage. It was no doubt through his influence that peace was preserved so long in Pennsylvania, not only between the Indians and settlers, but also between the Indians themselves, as he was emphatically a man of peace. Tammany is said to have resided at Shackamaxon, and to have been buried on the banks of the Neshaminy.

" Welcome, brothers! welcome to our shores !"
   Sedately spoke the king.
" We meet by council-fire to-day
   To hear what tidings you may bring
From o'er the waters far, far away.
   We listen, brothers, with attentive ear.
Speak, and keep naught back ;
   Speak, you've naught to fear !"

" Your greeting, brother, has touched the chord
   Of sympathy," said Penn, struggling to suppress
The feeling upgushing in his heart.
   " Brothers, fathers, words can ne'er express
The thoughts that echo through my mind.
   Brothers, that great Almighty Being,
He who formed the earth, the heavens above,
   The Wondrous, the Glorious, the All-Seeing ;
He whom you call Great Manitou ;
   He who hath written on those stars above,
And on the earth beneath our feet,—
   He there hath written of His marvellous love
Not only on the sun and earth without,
   But also on the soul within,—
'Tis this all-speaking, universal voice
   That makes the world all o'er akin.
That same Great Spirit whom you worship,
   Brothers, we likewise Him adore !
Listen, brothers ! 'Twas for the love of Him
   That we have sought your shore,
That we with you might find a home
   Wherein to dwell in love and peace.
Brothers, we cannot use the sword ;
   From war our God hath bid us cease,
And would have us cultivate
   Here in your beauteous land

The arts of peace and usefulness,—
Those arts which yield with bounteous hand
And bless mankind with plenty.
And, oh! brothers, may we remember ever,
As children of the God omnipotent,
The bond which binds our hearts together!"

When Penn his address concluded,
With great sedateness Tammany spoke:
"Fathers, to Brother Onas we have hearkened.
As from yon council-fire curls up the smoke
To heaven, so have our brother's weighty words
Ascended to the Spirit great and good.
To us they have been more than council-fire,—
They've been as life, and heat, and food.
Brother, with understanding you discourse.
When on this mission you were sent
Across the sounding, surging ocean,
Some good design was doubtless meant,
Some plan unseen to mortal ken.
To God's decree we humbly bend.
Tho' on those shores our fathers lie,
Yet westward on our way we'll wend,—
To the west our lands are bounded by the sun!
The red man, brother, you may trust;
For while the creeks and rivers run
The chain that binds us ne'er shall rust.
While the sun, the moon, the stars endure,
This treaty, made beside yon glist'ning stream,
Shall by our children's children sacred be;
And in the future it shall brightly gleam,
And shine afar o'er ages in the coming time!
Brothers, many years long past away,
A prophet-sage, beside this stream,
Saw in the visions to the dawning day.

He dreamed, yet it was not a dream :
    He saw the stranger o'er the bounding sea ;
He saw the red man leave this shore !
    To Fate we bend—'tis God's decree !"*

PART VIII.

Two hundred years ! Two hundred years
    Have lapsed in pulse of time !
That treaty made 'neath elm-tree's shade,†
    'Tis known in every clime.
To red men on the Western plain
    Tradition hath transmitted ;
The knowledge of that treaty's fame
    From Indian hath not flitted.
Whilst skimming o'er Ontario's wave,
    Or where Pacific's surges lave,
Transmitted forth from sire to son
    As legacy, each warrior gave
The honored name of William Penn,—
    The man of peace, the Indian's friend,
Whose loving faith in brother man
    Was steadfast to the end.

---

* It was a current tradition among the Indians two hundred years ago that a race of men from over the sea would dispossess them of their lands.

† Never, says Heckewelder, will the Delawares forget their elder brother Mignon, as they affectionately and respectfully call him. Between the years, he says, 1770 and 1780, they could relate very minutely what had passed between William Penn and their forefathers at their first meeting and afterwards.

This first meeting in 1682 was evidently a "league of friendship," which was repeated and confirmed afterwards. It was frequently alluded to at the different meetings between the Indians and the government of the Proprietor, as the records show. James Logan frequently alluded to that special treaty. On the 14th of Third month, 1721–22, he speaks of that "firm peace and league in these parts near forty years ago." At Conestoga, he speaks of it as "league of friendship and brotherhood with all the Indians then in these parts, and agreed that both you and his people should be all as one flesh and blood."

Two hundred years ! Two hundred years !
  What might they not have been,
If that great faith in brother man
  That throbbed in heart of Penn
Had throbbed in all mankind ?
  What dreadful wars, what horrid din,
The sabre's stroke, the tyrant's yoke,
  The seas of blood, all black with sin,
The bursting bomb that rent the air,
  And marked its track with death !
Fond woman's grief, strong man's despair,
  The soldier's shout, the cannon's breath,
Hot with its murderous vapor,
  The maddened thrust of maddened men,
The rending groan, the frenzied prayer,—
  All this, all this those years have seen !

Might have been ! O words abhorred !
  Ah ! man has deafened voice within,
And shocked with sounds discordant,
  O'erwhelming rude with crimson sin ;
Have idols reared and worshipping.
  Conscience, driven from her throne,
Patient sits with eyes o'erflown,
  Deserted, widowed, and alone !
Paradisic might have been the world,
  Use and Beauty have united wrought,
Adorned our earth with gems impearled.
  O Man ! who hath the treason taught,—
For thou alone the work hath marr'd,—
  Without thou hear'st gentle harmonies,
Within with deadly treason thou hast warr'd
  Against the heavenly symphonies.

Two hundred years ! Two hundred years !
  By rolling river's side,

In strength and beauty it appears,
   In glory and in pride.
The seeds of Freedom sown by Penn
   Struck deep in fertile ground ;
A strong and stalwart tree is seen,
   A nation great is spread around !
More glorious than the Pilgrims' shrine,
   Its record free from every stain,
No crimson blush of conscious shame
   Mantles Pennsylvania's fame.
TOLERATION reared her Ægis high,
   Inscribing first on Freedom's scroll,
Protecting every sect and creed,
   Securing freedom to the soul.

Two hundred years !   Two hundred years !
   On English soil is the Founder's tomb ;
His spirit's passed to heavenly spheres,
   Where flowers immortal bloom.
And that word he taught by lip and pen,
   Of spirit power and life,
Is needed in these present days
   Of selfish aim and strife.
Yes, that lucid calm of sweet content,
   As lived by William Penn,
Is needed in this restless age,
   Is needed now as then,
That life's great battle may be won,
   That PEACE may crown the end,
And conquest o'er material aims
   The closing scene attend.

AT OCEAN'S SIDE.

I sit beside the Ocean's side
And note each overflow,
As the wavelets to and fro
Move in concert with the tide.

With the pulses of the deep
Rhythmic motion thus they keep,
Every wavelet being one,
As is all beneath the sun.

Every star which shines afar
Moves in rhythm as they blend,
Each with all, without an end,
. Without a break, without a jar.

Thus are Nature's motions clear:
Echoes break upon the ear
From the depths of Ocean's cave
As on each shore its waters lave.

Thus in every guise we find surprise,
A mystery in the sea !
All her movements thus agree,
As the stars which greet our eyes.

In heaven above, in earth below,
On mountain heights, in streamlet's flow,
A wond'rous harmony is seen,—
A silver cord, a golden mean.

NATURE'S TEACHING.

To roam with Nature through the groves,
  And o'er the fields and plains,
To gather roses free from thorns
  In life's sequestered, grassy lanes !
To roam with thee, O Solitude,
  To listen to thy murmurs low,
Thy melodies that thrill the soul
  With gentle numbers as they flow,
Meandering in their course,
From some mysterious source !

II

When, by Contemplation led,
  With Nature thus we stray,
What is it that inspires the soul
  To soar from earth away ?
That lifts the mind, impels the thought
  To roam thro' other spheres,
As the eaglet, soaring high
  Above life's cares and fears ?
Does some angelic spirit bright
Thus fill the mind with mystic light ?

Whence, O Solitude, thy inspiration ?
  Do the anthems of the mighty past
At times impress our souls
  With thoughts of glorious cast,

7*

Sculptured after perfect models?
　Or, when distant from the haunts of men,
Alone with Nature by the sounding sea,
　In meadow, grotto, field, or glen,
By mountain-side or on the flowery lea,
With thought and mind and fancy free,

IV.

What hand sweeps o'er the heart-strings,
　Attuning all to sweetest melody,
All sounds discordant hushed
　Or changed to heavenly harmony?
Ecstatic raptures fill the mind
　And flood the soul with joy;
'Lone peace and happiness we find,
　Without discordancy to cloy
Our feelings, or with fetters bind
The thoughts that echo through the mind.

V.

O Man! when thus alone with Nature,
　Naught near but the unseen air
Sweeping thro' the crimson forests,
　Resounding fill thy ear
With notes of gentle music;
　Or in the sweetly-scented spring,
As in a dream thou goest forth,
　Wandering to greet the day-king
As he courses on his flight,
Ere he leaves thee in the arms of night.

VI.

And balmy, soft-breathed breezes
　Fan thy cheek and wake the sod
Beneath thy feet to life and beauty,
　And Nature's worship ascendeth unto God

With melody, and all created things rejoice
In sunshine, gushing warm and bright,
Whispering, speaking with all-mighty voice
To sun and earth, *Let there be light !*
And forth it beams, O ray sublime !
That gushes from a font divine.

VII.

O Light ! thou parent of Heat
And Sunshine, 'tis in spring-time
That we prize and bless thee most.
'Tis then thy ray sublime,
Bright in its glorious revelation,
As when God's angel, girt with light
And clad with creative power,
Banished by a spell of might,
Wafted to the chambers of the night,
And breath'd o'er earth a holy light.

VIII.

Scientists and seers would track thy course,
And wander o'er regions of infinity
To trace thee to thy phosphoric source,
Ascribing to some unknown affinity
Of sun and earth thy marvellous ray.
Science can probe the earth, and o'er
The depths of mighty ocean lay
Her bounds from shore to shore,
And pour her voice unceasingly
Throughout the caverns of the sea.

IX.

But can she analyze thy piercing glance,
That beam'st forth august, sublime ?
Thou smile of heaven, transfusing space,
And lighting worlds by power divine.

O ray immortal ! shadow of infinity !
   Thou that flittest through the spheres,
Comrade and compeer of eternity,
   By time unaltered, unchanged by years !
And, O Man, is no revelation from afar
Conveyed by yonder twinkling star ?

x.

That thou mayst know and tell
   When thus alone in solitude,
In summer's heat, in winter's cold,
   Or in the solemn autumn's quietude ?
When in the forest's shades thou roamest,
   With bright banners waving o'er thy head,
Their trophies of the summer past,
   Their golden banners fringed with red,
Wafting, drifting here and there,
Streaming in the autumnal air ?

XI.

Or when winter binds the streams
   And checks their source,
And northern gales career
   Relentless in their course ?
Then wrap the robes of winter
   'Round thy form and wander forth,
With no companion but the ice-king,—
   That despot of the North,
Who rules with frigid breath
His region of the earth.

XII.

If thy soul is thus awakened
   On the mountain's height or ocean's shore,
If in the war of elementary strife
   Thou hearest music in the roar

And battle of the raging elements,—
  Gold may not, perchance, be thine,
Yet thou art rich, art Nature's child,
  Inheritor of gifts sublime !
Thine are the mountains, and the valleys thine,
Though not recorded in the book of Time.

XIII.

Thy treasures are immortal treasures.
  The narrow and contracted soul
May see no use in God's profuseness,
  May hear no music roll from pole to pole,
May sneer at truth and beauty,
  May treasure earth by what she yields,
May close his eye to Nature's rarity,—
  The senseless idiot judges as he feels !
His ear is shut to that immortal Voice
  That makes thy heart, thy soul rejoice !

TO ELLEN H. PAUL.

THE circling years each other meet,
Unending Time makes all complete;
In form and substance they appear,
Revolving round their central sphere.
Fourscore and ten! how great the span
Which circles in the life of man!
When thou wast young Columbia's fame
Was just baptized in Freedom's name;
And dull the pace and slow the speed
Of postman then on back of steed.
Now lightning sends the thoughts we feel,
And coursers swift on roads of steel
Speed o'er the land with quicken'd pace,
As though their life was in the race.
And since upon thy father's knee
Thou sat, beneath the spreading tree,
How many changes Time has wrought!
The shadowed past, how full of thought!
In early youth thou wast a bride,—
Yes, dearly loved, thy James's pride.
And we, his friends and thine, are near
This eve to greet thy natal year!
Fourscore and ten! how great indeed,
How passing strange the life we lead.

How like a dream the past appears
To manhood's prime or lengthened years!
I backward gaze : the past recalls
A youthful form who loved these halls
A friend of mine—in school-boy days
We wandered forth 'midst Pleasure's maze,—
A son of thine, whose cheery face
Time and years can ne'er erase
Whilst time and reason hold their place !
Surrounded thus with memories sweet,
Old friends, this evening here we meet.
Eternal mind knows not of death ;
She passeth not with parting breath.
If so, these halls of quarried stone
Were more than Thought or Reason's throne,
Were more than Art, which gave them form.
Not so our dead we hopeless mourn ;
For, though in spirit or in flesh,
Communing thus we would refresh
Each heart immersed in daily care,
Secure each bliss that each can bear,
Without e'en grief, without e'en care !
Transposing this in highest sense,
Translating it as permanence,
Let Joy pulsate in every heart,
With blithesome cheer and woman's art !
For thou wast born in month of June,
'Midst birdlings' songs of sweetest tune,
In crowning month of blessed spring,
Whose floral offering here we bring,
Blest flowers, all radiant in their bloom,
Breathing low their sweet perfume,—
Rose and orange freshly blown
Since the morning sun hath shone.
Thus flow'rets wreathe thy years with joy,
Thy ninety years without alloy !

THE "BOSTON."*

A WIFE'S VISION.

I STRAIN my eyes across the deep,
  I listen as each courier rings,
  And hope the tidings that he brings
With joy may make my pulses leap.

I listened with a hope deferred
  To catch some tidings from the brave
  Who sailed athwart the eastern wave.
Alas! my heart with fear is stirred.

As every rumor from afar,
  Each breath from off the stormy sea,
  Alas! alas! they all agree,
And every gleam of hope they mar.

My children ask with tearful eye
  The fearful question, Will he come
  And cheer again a happy home?
Alas! each shadow sailing by

---

* The loss of the "Boston" created, at the time, a profound impression.
She sailed from Glasgow, and was never heard of afterwards. It is supposed
that she was wrecked by icebergs.

O'er my heart their terrors cast,—
  I feel the iceberg's chilling breath.
  O God ! it was a fearful death,
In ocean's solitudes so vast.

Not always thus, for yesternight
  A vision gleamed upon my sight
  With a subdued and mellowed light,
And clearer than the noonday bright.

A bark with spreading sail I saw ;
  I heard the sailors' cheerful note,
  The welcome from the cannon's throat,
And woke amid the loud huzza !

8

THE LIGHT OF LIFE.

COMMUNE with me, transcendent guest;
　　For thou hast promised as reward,—
　　As to disciple from his Lord,—
That all are doubly blessed

Who seek, as Grecian Socrates,
　　Thy gift of inward light.
　　For sweetness, pure and bright,
Blend with thy philosophies.

O calm and tranquil light !
　　Which flows from blissful sea,
　　Flow on so great and free,
From sunlit fountain bright,

That all the world may learn
　　Thy power to bless and save,
　　As ship on ocean's crested wave
To Master's hand doth turn.

Thou blessed hope of all mankind,
　　Attuned to Reason's voice !
　　For all may make their choice,
And way to Life may find.

Eternal beacon on the shore
　　Of Time's relentless wave,
　　Where frosted waters curling lave
With an uneasy roar.

But through the darkness and the din
  Still shines that beacon-light,
  Through the mist and gloom of night,
Responsive to a voice within.

Another voice of love and cheer
  The listening ear hath heard ;
  In blending *Oneness* to the Word
'Tis found, distinct and clear.

THIS is no death.   The sun goes down behind the western
 hills
In beauty and in grandeur, and in brightness clad.
So rests, so sinks the soul that trusts in God.   His will it
 wills,·
And, like the sun, again shall rise, and making glad
With sheen effulgent, with loveliest and with fairest zone !
 Yes, like the sun, immortal, with career of light,
Thy course, O soul that trusts in God alone,
 Shall be as one who walks by faith and not by sight.

This is no death.   God's law perfects the soul that loveth
 Him,
 And lifts him into fairer, nobler scenes of love and joy,
Where angels and where seraphs breathe the song of praise
 and hymn
 In notes celestial, in anthem without alloy !

Then move our souls, O Father, " with divine unrest !"
 For, as one of old ⁕ hath said, no power we know
Save Thine to fill us with the holiest and the best,
 No power save Thine alone aside can throw
Time's burden of distress.   Pressed down are we with care
 At times, with sorrow, and with groundless fear ;
And, though the sky above is now so fair and bright,·
 To-morrow's sun may find us with a listless sense and
 deafened ear

⁕ Æschylus, B.C. 500.

To all harmonious sounds, and weaken'd eye see not the
    light
  Of Thy effulgent grace and truth. Thus, thus we learn to
    walk the way
Of right, and not of strength or wealth, or power or might
  Of man. 'Tis thus we learn to want, to wait, to watch, to
    pray.

Thus rest doth come, sweet rest! the rest of Faith and Hope.
  Victorious thus o'er Death ; no more oppressed
With strife, of loss or gain. Thus can we cope
  With our dread foe, thus be at rest !

TO M. AND R.

Of a fourfold love secure,
Dearest children, you are sure,—
Father, mother, always near,
Guarding you from every fear.

And grandma, too, with love imbued,
Securing you from tempests rude ;
Her faithful heart and watchful eye,
A tender love, is ever nigh.

Thus, beneath the same home-tree,
May heart, and hand, and mind agree,
That love abound and discord flee,
In harmony and melody.

And tho' the year just passed away
Has palled the sight with mantle gray ;
A cheery glance that met its dawn,
A loving smile and voice is gone !

An aching void is left behind
In every heart, in every mind.
Dearest children, this we mourn.
Thus in life and love we learn

To place our hopes beyond the grave,—
To trust in grace, its power to save,
That we may meet with those above
Again in courts of heavenly love.

LINCOLN AND LIBERTY.

LINES WRITTEN ON HEARING THAT CALIFORNIA HAD
VOTED FOR LINCOLN IN 1864.

FROM where the placid Delaware winds onward in its course,
To where Niagara's waters flow with their resistless force ;
From where New England's stalwart sons, amidst the woods
  of Maine,
The axe rings forth the anthem, rings forth the glad refrain !

The miner in the land of Penn, the boatman at the oar,
The farmer in the teeming West, among his garnered store,
The sailor on the ocean, amidst the surging sea,
All, all have caught the glad acclaim,—LINCOLN and LIB-
  ERTY !

And where Columbia's patriot sons encamp at Richmond's
  gate,
Their every shot and every shell proclaim the voice of fate !
"The slave's dull ear" has caught the note, the anthem of
  the free,
As Dahlgren's voice pronounces clear,—LINCOLN and LIB-
  ERTY !

'Twas thus along our country's shore from heart to heart it
  flew ;
The lightning's wing conveyed the news that gladdened not a
  few.

All o'er the land, from lake to gulf, responsive thrilled each
    breast,—
From North to South, from sea to sea, and in the "fair
    young West."

And o'er Pacific's gentle wave, far toward the setting sun,
From where the sands with gold are mixed, and silvery
    waters run ;
From where Nevada rears his head, and Winter's chaplet
    crowns ;
Where Nature, both in mount and tree, in giant growth
    abounds,—

There, in that land where Broderick lived, there where he
    fought and fell,
In Freedom's ranks his friends have ranged, and Freedom's
    cohorts swell !
The tide from out the Golden Gate is ebbing toward the
    sea ;
Amidst the shrouds the sailor sings,—LINCOLN and LIBERTY !

TO THE COMET OF 1882.

"Earth shook, red meteors flashed along the sky,
And conscious Nature shuddered at the cry."—*Campbell.*

WHAT portent dire dost thou inspire?
Forebodest danger?
Where thy altar, whence thy fire,
Mysterious stranger?

Comest thou in mirth to greet the earth
As rocket through the sky?
Or is it wrath that gave thee birth,—
Vengeance from on high?

In these, our times, must man's fell crimes
In channels backward flow?
Art thou as knell to chant the chimes
Of pestilence and woe?

Yoke to thy car. "Is't rampant war?"
Foretell'st of the time
That seers have seen in visions far,
When man was ripe with crime?

Nay! earth is not by heaven forgot;
God's blessings onward flow,
And man has much yet in his lot
Of happiness below.

Yon star, which flew with radiant hue
    The spheres among,
Of time foretold which man shall view
    That poet-peasant sung,—

" That sense and worth o'er a' the earth"
    Shall be enthroned,
And vice and crime, where'er their birth,
    Shall be disowned.

LINES

DEDICATED TO THE MEMORY OF PEMBERTON HALLO-
WELL, WHOSE REMAINS LIE INTERRED IN THE ABING-
TON FRIEND'S GRAVEYARD.

THERE, in the shade of that gigantic tree
    Which rears its branches to the sky,
There, 'neath the sod and fragrant lea,
    With tears sincere and heartfelt sigh,

We laid thee there, without one word
    By priest or prophet spoken :
Affection's sigh was only heard,—
    A mute but fitting token.

Friend of my youth, we gave to thee
    No costly tomb or lettered urn,
Naught but the sod and spreading tree,
    The simple stone and ripened fern.

What need we more? " Can animated bust
    Back to its mansion call the fleeting breath ?"
What need we more than filial trust
    To meet the messenger of death ?

What more than this can creed impart
    To that which God has given ?
No monkish faith or priestly art
    Can bar the path to heaven.

NOVEMBER'S IDES.

(1868.)

O PATRIOT sons of patriot sires,
Breathe in our souls your fond desires!
You strove to save from traitorous foes
Columbia from unnumbered woes.

And, ye martyred host on high,
Do you in spirit hover nigh,
To touch our hearts with patriot fire,
Attune our souls to Freedom's lyre!

So that November's thoughtless throngs
May not forget your countless wrongs,
And that you trod the blood-stained path
To save the land from righteous wrath.

That blood-stained path where Lyon led,
Where Baker fell and Lincoln bled,—
A blood-stained path it was, in truth,
To hoary sire and generous youth.

And may the land you died to save
Forget not what you martyrs gave!
You coined your hearts and gave your all,
Inspired your thought at duty's call.

For now beneath September's sky,
When shadows flit and clouds pass by;
When misty vapors wrap us round,
Masking form and muffling sound ;

When the leaves have reached their prime,
In our quiet autumn time,—
Now the fitting time for thought,
By the ripening seasons brought.

So may our country's crisis near
Bring to the freedman's heart no fear,
But hope and joy in every eye
As blithely past the tidings fly.

From lake to lake to ocean's wave,
Where the chafing waters lave ;
From Mississippi's ceaseless font
To the mountains of Vermont ;

From the Gulf to Golden Gate,
All o'er the land, from State to State,
Conveyed by magic flame aslant,
Ablaze with light, the name of GRANT !

TO THE MEMORY OF C. HOWARD COMLY.

In the spring-time of life,
  When existence is joy,
When Hope fills the heart
  Without an alloy ;

When each pulse is a throb
  Of youthful delight,
When unconscious of aught
  That can sully or blight ;

When friend and acquaintance
  Were hopeful of thee,
Ah ! who of the present
  This end could foresee ?

Thou comest, O Death !
  With thy scythe and thy dart,
Wounding and crushing
  And wrenching apart.

O sorrow, how deep !
  For the living we mourn,
For hearts that are weary,
  With anguish o'erborne.

For thee, dearest Howard,
   In the haven of rest,
With naught to disquiet,
   With naught to molest.

Thus, with trust in our hearts,
   With our hearts we believe.
For the living we mourn,
   For the living we grieve.

THE END.

www.ingramcontent.com/pod-product-compliance
Lightning Source LLC
Chambersburg PA
CBHW022149020726
47496CB00008B/2626